LOVE LIES
IN THE
THROES OF
RHETORIC

LOVE LIES IN THE THROES OF RHETORIC

ANTHONY GEDELL

NEW YORK   LOS ANGELES

Jacket Copyright 2024 by Winding Road Stories
Interior Design: A Raven Design
ISBN#: 978-1-960724-28-1 (pbk)
ISBN#: 978-1-960724-29-8 (ebook)

Published by Winding Road Stories
www.windingroadstories.com

For to him that is joined to all the living there is hope: for a living dog is better than a dead lion. For the living know that they shall die: but the dead know not any thing, neither have they any more a reward; for the memory of them is forgotten. Also their love, and their hatred, and their envy, is now perished; neither have they any more a portion for ever in any *thing* that is done under the sun.

~ ECCLESIASTES 9:4 (KJV)

If you're here, c'est la vie, hallelujah. From me to you. Hallelujah. Thus enter the abyss. Lasciate ogne speranza, voi ch'intrate. Everything a wasteland, all paradises lost, journey to the end of that long and cold lonely night. These are desperate times. Turn the page. The story never ends. Turn the page. The story keeps on keeping on. The family never dies. The human family. From me to you. You gazing back at me. That rubied jewel hung banging in our chests. Red sky over our bones, rust pervading every horizon. The achromatic gloom never ceasing, thunder in the clouds of our lungs. Let me tell you a story. Hence adjourned in council are we around a small and fervent smoldering over coals in evolutionary repose by solemnity refusal of the diamond. It does not mean the teller is alive at the end of it, nor so the story concluded in death. There's liberation to that. Writing amongst the dead. Let me tell you a story. Are you listening? From me to you with that love. Nothing but love. Spread it along. Pass it on. Turn the page.

PART 1

When she cried she got headaches. She was crying, he was apologizing. It was the last thing he wanted to do.

"The best apology is a change in habits," she says.

Her name is Eudora, his Trasc. He feels like he's been here before. Would love her in every life.

"We're too young to feel this old. Too old to die young," Eudora says. She massages her temples.

Trasc sits bowed and silent. Reaches for her toes to rub out the pain in her head. She pulls away. The lake breeze weaves its way through the small and haggard iniquitous cathedral of aching that has become their home. His hands throb to be thrown through something. String up his own cold heart and go a few rounds.

All the gale about this twirling sphere are small hymns of gasping sorrow. Heavy wind wheezes upon the dark and lonely streets of Lake Hopatcong. Apothecary and hoarder of such long darknesses shunning away incendiary light.

No power yet in the house. Was owned by someone on Eudora's side. Finding something affordable, available, and fit to occupy something like looking for Eden. Firelight surrounding them beset in mourning. Sacrificial torment to love lost.

The candle flame vested upon the coffin walls surrounding them paints Eudora in shadow of some dogged beast. Swallowed by her own silhouette. A spectral metamorphosis divulged by the fractures of her own heart. Too much time and too much pain. In her chest resides the celestial gravel mined from dead stars. The poison seeping through the cracks of glaciers.

This woman could kill me, Trasc thinks. *What have we become? The monster I created. This woman can eat me alive.*

He was always too intuitive for his own good. Made him seem cynical where he wasn't. Made him right for the job. Both jobs. Zero sum occupational hazards. Made him feel alone and petrified.

"I'm scared. I don't know what to do. I just want to go home," Trasc says.

"Whose fault is that?"

"That's what you say to a friend? After everything we've been through?"

"That what we are, bestie?"

"That's cold. Just cold."

"That's me. Cold. Ice cold, baby. I'm tired of being your mother. I'm tired of being."

"Don't talk that way."

"Nobody is listening."

"I'm listening."

"Same as nobody."

"We had a good day. Didn't we have a good day?"

"Oh, sure. I had a blast. Wow. What a gas. That's all there is to it, right? Eating, drinking, and fucking."

"Are you okay?"

"I'm fine."

"You used to not be this way. Used to not talk this way."

"Go on and tell me about myself. Shape me into this image of me. All these perceptions coming home to roost."

"This wave of sadness and disappointment washes over you. You're drowning. You won't take my hand and you won't acknowledge the waves. Emotions should be like weather, Eu. If those clouds aren't moving you need to consider their weight and what they carry."

"There he is. The talker. All these years. Blah, blah, blah."

"I'll listen."

"Nobody listens. Nobody gives a shit what anybody is saying. Nobody. Count your blessings and you tally up the losses you can endure. Just circling the drain. Should have quit while we were ahead."

"I can't quit you."

"Oh, you boy. Boy, boy, boy."

"This boy shit again. Am I not man enough? What is a man?"

"When I find one, I'll let you know."

"Fuck you, Eudora."

Trasc contemplates the shadows. The rhythms and hums of the apathetic dark that flows through the woven trails. Kinship to the ocean that has risen without warrant to congeal the incandescent land in the jaws of a god to serpents. Only the population in this desolate visage can remove the rock of such caves to set forth this resurrected flowing.

"Hallelujah," he says. "It's over at last. This whole big nothing."

"What does that mean?"

"It means that I don't want to be here anymore."

"Don't keep saying that. You can't keep saying that. If you keep saying it, I'll do it."

"Don't talk like that."

She laughs.

"What?"

"I guess that's our problem."

"What is?"

"We don't talk."

"About what?"

"Anything. We don't talk about fucking anything."

Architectural values of manmade shelter stand upon the woven trails like tombstones. So much life paired to silence. He knows every word they beckon will be heard by the suburban psychopaths surrounding them. So packed yet so desolate.

The air moves with violence descending from a full black sky. Nothing natural about it. Not moving through the streets but pressing down a void of gaping emptiness. A vacuum where the brightest star was sucking it all away. The stomachs of the alone and the hungry of all the timid souls hiding in murderous trembling.

"We don't belong here. This is a vacation spot. Or at least a once was kind of one, clouded with amnesia. These chasm homes. This place just slowly fading away. Nothing but uppity white folk, Eu. Those some seasick anvil eyes and sunken faces out there. Like they ain't ever looked at no sun in their life. Like they aren't healthy. Things of another species. When shit hits the fan and we are just about as northbound as can be it'll be tough to get out this place. Probably might just be best to be still. This ain't no refuge. No home."

"Who pays for this home?"

"That roof we left was the only one I ever put up over my head. Only one I ever had."

"How long are you going to use that?"

"Use what?"

"Your victim card."

"We lost our jobs. Our money. Our home. Maybe done up

and lost our damn minds. This whole country just about screwed off their very own heads."

"Boohoo. It was tragic and mysterious and sexy when I met you. Now it's just pathetic. You're going to be thirty. Hard to tell. Sometimes you can be such a child."

He always considered she was too young for him. A five-year difference lay as too young eyes lost in the valleys of a face with all the etchings and illusory incisions of time passing.

His tongue osculates in his mouth for a drink. The anger he'd tried to mend and bury out back coming up like an old friend. For what it might be worth to any debt collecting angel mortgaging space in the sky any sense of spiritual growth was a combine in backwards motion. This graveyard of past selves we leave behind.

Eudora rises from the couch. It seemed she'd taken the measures of standing upright only out of habit these days. A heaviness in her movements. Gone to a land of pirouetting corpses was her glow of youth stuck between something like a cracked windshield bathed in the shadow of incoming red lights and a parasite. She'd sometimes resemble to him something tossed out the window of a moving vehicle and run over by another. Just kept on spinning down a glass riddled road all torn up and abandoned and in ruin. Every word shrill and resuscitated out of her.

There was nothing to be found but tragedy there in that youth. Something like digging a hole at a crossroads and planting a white flag.

A resentment has built between them over the years. Severed mending by laziness, time and exposure, and the poverty of their reliance. It came in the form of petty sympathy and self-hatred. Thinking they had blown up their world. Thinking that they might have been happier someplace else. Like some other life out there away from him would save her from herself. They did not govern themselves in the way time abided these earthly fears and delights. Indifferent submission to gracefully loving the one they got and working on their bond. It hadn't occurred to them that it was something to be worked at.

She makes her way into the bathroom through the labyrinth of boxes and downed consumeristic means that had taken hold of their lives in the move. High school sweethearts racing toward a redlight. Penniless and on the run. Jobless, world-weary, desperate from the fight. A future enveloped by arrears and evictions.

Parts of the shore they left chased out others. All the rivers running into the sea. Small towns and highways as canals. Harbingering sorrowful tales of terribleness in parts of Florida, Louisiana, Maine, California. The world kept spinning all clogged up.

He considers these not dystopian times. The dystopia was all around you, in you. Lurking around every corner and in every heart. The dystopia was always and it is people. Trasc had just been about ready to bow out of this human predicament ahead of the curtain. He'd always felt the flood coming. It seemed to him that people welcomed the collapse and the carrying out such decree.

It was all one single genealogy. He imagined a wheel of life where upon entering this carousel of incubation a small hand dipped in a vat of blood and fingerprinted.

Forever in each end never a new beginning. Only ceaseless start overs. The many times a world can die. All these new and shining plagues. Closer the tide, he thought that even a world commits suicide. He tries to shake away the bad thoughts like spiders. Drive the snakes back under their rocks.

Trasc got good at leaving things behind. All but a memory. He remembers the lightness of her the first time she'd stepped into that old apartment. Dancing naked in the kitchen making eggs for them they'd end up not eating. There'd be other things to devour. He would often reconcile the very idea that he'd not seen her dance in years now. He'd wonder many times in his life thinking about women and trying to brood himself from his own consciousness to solve this murder of existence if she was faith or fathom. To know a loss such as this and witness something beautiful come to grief.

This solitary moment together. He'd remember it as a blessing. Too much time taking things for granted. An all too late penance. Cast out to a sick bed holding his own bleeding heart. These family circles and spiraling, endless desires. Only questions and departures. Running from a shadow in which he knows the shape but not its name. All that lay ahead is the long impotent line to toe. Faithful to his isolation. Escape was no longer an option. Any road ahead was only a valley unto a cliff. He never had authority over his own life. To what means was he to make amends having burned every bridge.

Eudora out of habit flicks the switch of the bathroom to no availing light. Trasc remains frozen in the wavering luster. He immobilizes himself in times like this. Shuts down with an inability to move on from the worst. A disastrous and perfidious affair with catastrophizing and selfish indolence.

He sets his eyes on the desk Eudora had surprised him with and built him. He came home to the apartment with her laying on top of it. They almost broke the thing that night. Now it lay in pieces in the corner of the room from last night's tantrum. She'd been drinking and got violent like that.

He had heard before never to trust a blonde. Hard to say Eudora was anything of such. She'd now taken the appearance of a mugshot. Gold flecked blue eyes holding antique worlds inside those two relic lamps all burnt out.

Hair a thin, ashy weave of some combination of colors residing on a wheel of lamentation.

Eudora starts the shower concealed away in the cold dark. The hot water heater down below the house is broken. Trasc couldn't fix it. Had no idea his way around the thing. He would come to think of himself as an unable practitioner of needless idealism with no practical tools to provide any use to anybody. He would take cold showers. Moments and ticking seconds in life cascading by him as irritations. A fitting in of the basic functions needed to lug around this rotting jerky. Eudora used to not be able to withstand such low temperatures. Doesn't make a sound.

She would do this often. Trailing off with no word or announcement. Trasc gets to his feet. The house stands as coliseum to their desolate lonesomeness. It eased him in his entry of the house to see the photographs hanging from wall to wall over the single couch that occupied half the room. Pictures of Eudora and him. She'd been working doubles nonstop. It became an inability to complete small tasks and he became inattentive and unavailable.

He steps closer to the wall. The running water and old pipes the only thing occupying the silent valleys of this suburban jungle. Cold air rises from walls he feels as though he can poke holes through. He scales them as some timeline chronicling an unbecoming.

Twelve pictures in sum hung on a string of dead Christmas lights. Further and further they drift apart in each passing photograph as he goes down the line. Never many of them. Any other person of merit is someone who needs to be held on to. Pictures of Eudora holding her niece and nephew. Everybody just started distancing themselves. Something seems to leave Eudora right through the eyes with each passing photograph. Like a diseased brain in the young. It wasn't anything magical but rather a literal sense and pictograph of the thing. Trasc steps out on to the stoop when he hears the shower run dry. He would get anxious anytime he had to be around her. Anytime she called. She was always sinking. The house began to feel too tight. His clothes felt tight. His skin. His life. Repercussions to his codependency.

Small yard fenced by a weathered white picket. It shakes in the wind with warnings of giving way. Wood rot and mosquito gargling sensorial in the dark. The front light bears no wick and no bulb. Something moves in the yard right of him stage to an abandoned house. Large sums of jilted quarters twisting away in these concrete labyrinths paired to desperate mysteries no longer inhabiting them.

Staring out into the dark all that he could think of were hauntings. Something adjacent to his being. Settlement upon a notion that you pay an expense at the rate of your lies.

Different shades of blackness in the sky swirling revelations. He can see but a few feet in front of him. A stillness to the cold where the wind can be heard but seldom felt. A steel sign rattles on the lone tree in the yard. The house's previous occupants desired domestic housekeeping. Wanted to let everybody know they had guns.

Concealed carry state now. The house was in bad shape when he first saw it. Second time up this way. Driving through the outskirts of the wild ghettos of abandoned provinces. A kid was left alone inside. The mother chasing a fix. Kid got hold of one of the guns and used it on himself. The boy could not have been any older than seven. Didn't have a bedroom of his own in the house.

Now remained a landscape pillaged of its interiorities. Days of nothing wandering this stray dog world. Pile on pile of the bitter and the dreary. Minds sailing an upside-down Viking's funeral just all of it gone and adrift.

Somebody whistles a tune on down the road. Wandering light small and swaying pirouettes through the splitting shadows. A man holds the artificial glow and breathes hard in his advancing. No level slope along this entanglement for the impotent. No right turn on these coiling roads. He is whistling Deck the Halls. When he walks on by the road Trasc makes through brush that will need tending lining his fence a grown man unkept with facial hair wearing a shirt of an old children's cartoon talking to himself. Trasc tries to greet him. Been experiencing this more and more in this country. When he speaks calm, fluid, and complete sentences to another person it seems as though he speaks in unknown tongues. The man moves on gibbering with his pants sagging no more a trodden infant and fugitive to unknown asylums.

It seemed to Trasc early on there was something in the water here. It wasn't a stretch. The mailbox was filled with letters and warnings. Boiling the water that ran from those pipes still unsafe. They were lucky to have well water.

Trasc pans his head side to side. Two small panels of mulch with neglected plants shed the last of their liveries. He had planted them the last time he was at the house.

The silence reveals different levels and depths to him. Stranger in a strange land, terrain still foreign and remote. A traveler this way of miniscule sum. Dying summer upon his introduction. There was a hot and wild feeling in the chest. It reminded him of the Staten Island blackouts when he was a kid. There was something sinister in the elements of this place.

His own weakness sickens him. An avalanche in his gut. It's time to leave this place. Salvage to the insane. The broken hearted and shattered dreams. He backs away inside.

Full black. The candles all blown out but two. Eudora had gone to bed. The proximity of the infrastructure can be taken in from the doorway. Pale flame flags peeling along the walls and around the bedroom door. Eudora is sitting up in bed staring at the wall wrapped up inside all that dark and fire.

She reminded him of certain violences countries learned from other countries in what she learned from him. Trasc considered what they were into and the symmetries in our societal accumulation of trauma and dread under a cracked sky hung insular as a banner of surrender. He could not sacrifice his selfishness to provide something more to her that would pull her out of the severity of her impossible sadness.

Distant lonely sounds over black hills. To him everything laid waste. It was hard to see anything but a drowned future.

"It's early," Trasc says.

"I have to get up early."

"What time are you working?"

"Open to close."

"What time?"

"Sun up to sun down. Who's counting?"

"You sure are keeping score."

"Could use a victory."

"I know."

"You're not staying."

"I can't."

"You can't."

"This could be a big break for me. For us. This case. I got a guy who'll get me on. Believe that? Like we talked about. Done with bullshit jobs."

"You can't be done with what you can't keep."

"The police ain't working. We always say a writer is a detective. Why not put something to use of this worthless obsession."

Eudora laughs. Her little teeth show like fangs. Lips coiling into a tight and sinister beckoning of curdling judgments. If there was something in her smile to reach her gaze the wiring was all wrong and the roads and valleys on her face were a perfidious composition of her own neurotic behaviors.

"You'll be late to a murder. You a detective. The world really is coming to an end."

"Tomorrow is what? How many in a row?"

"What?"

"Doubles."

"It's good money."

"It's not worth it."

"To somebody who has not a sense of worth for responsibility."

"I'll find a job when I come up here. I can help. You can depend on me."

She laughs.

"What," he says.

"The sink's busted."

"Save these idle hands. I'll pick up a trade."

"You can do anything."

"Please."

"We haven't been a part this long. This place will be underwater inside of ten years. And we all will be holding each other's heads under the currents."

"I thought we weren't keeping count."

"That's just keeping score. I'd have ended the game sooner."

"Look at this place. It's worse off than most of the homes they just let stand and rot around here."

"You're not the one who stays here. All alone."

"It was supposed to be better. Being near your family."

"For them."

"It'll all be washed away. We can get back to the way things used to be. Remember that love. Nothing but that love. Wanting to do right by each other. We ain't done yet. I caused us a lot of stress. Triggers and pressures. I'm trying not to be that guy anymore. It will all be washed clean."

"Here's to not being around to see the changes."

"Stop saying shit like that. Just stop."

"My dad will be up to work on the place. You don't need to worry about a thing."

"What's that supposed to mean?'

"It means you're useless."

Trasc believes these words and within them bows out.

"Remember when we almost got that camper to live in?" Eudora says.

"All we can afford."

"All I can afford."

"You changed your mind. After going out in your sister's. You didn't have a good time. You have to find a pocket of happiness in every day. You're not trying."

"The brakes broke. Shaun had to fix them. There I was thinking can't do this either. My boy wouldn't know the steering wheel from the exhaust."

"If I'm so pitiful why don't you tell me to leave."

"You don't have the balls to leave."

"Ask me to leave, Eudora."

Trasc grabs the duffel bag at his feet.

"What do you care about that stupid job. It's a hotel."

"I have had a hard life. Everyday..."

"This again. Here's to a time around the sun where you won't just age. You'll grow up," Eudora blows out the candle bedside. One remains alight. She lays on her side turning her back to him.

"I haven't had a drink in two weeks."

"I liked you better when you were drinking. You weren't such a pussy. Had moxy. Some edge. Now you just betray yourself talking all the time. Ain't much the silent type no more. This God-fearing crap. I think the worst part of me is you. Worst part is that I know you. Even if you want to forget. You can't stand me for it."

"This is absurd."

"Isn't it."

"You've been trying to push me away."

"That bad?"

"Life is bulk mindset. You are in control of the colors of your own mind. We can flick the switch. Enjoy the company of one another. I go back and I read our letters. It is meant to be worked on. Our bond. We can make it strong. Carry each other's burdens."

"I'm going to bed."

"Look…"

Eudora sticks her face in a pillow and screams.

"I said that I am exhausted and that I am going to bed. You want to go on and on and on. You're talking to yourself."

"Feels that way."

"Leave or get out. Shut the door."

"We're all we got, Eu."

"Pity."

"What are we doing."

"Dying. Now go. Blow the last candle out."

TWO

Out of the house and into the yard. Total dark envelopes Trasc. Such a silence he'd like to seek shelter in more than reconcile with. He might as well be on the dark side of the moon. He steps to and squares up with a tree in the yard and starts throwing haymakers until the pain in his hands mend the pain inside.

Single bag lone wolf traveler. The clothes inside no more or less a luxury than the bag that they're in. In the dark he can still make out characteristics of the world. The emotional resolutions and essences of a place molded by shadows. Outlined are declarative natures of the expensive overheads those around him lived under.

Stranger in a strange land. Multiple cars. Houses presenting themselves as galas, balls, events. Trailers and pools. Trasc would scrounge around for loose change just to make gas. Knew the car he drove was not a man's car. His only pair of boots scuffed and torn by aggressive work. One boot barely laced. Always living in and out of packaging. He'd felt he had a good run but was running on fumes toward only fires querying every destination.

Colder outside than how he should feel. She'd be crying herself to sleep. He knows this. It sits between barbed-wired ribs deep within his sternum the cold hard truth that he cannot be without her. He no longer knew how to be alone. It wasn't so that he could not live without her but in such that he could not survive. He wasn't sure if the survival was meant to be with her or done so by her in such that he would be able to get on living his charmed and atavistic life while she slowly capsized into herself buried inside her own grave while her hands reached out not to dig herself out but to offer them up to those around her until final descent.

That too long relationship at the ripe wrong age that leaves men playing catchup to desire left with an unquenchable thirst for women. Feeling as though something was owed to him. Something better. In that he wore out the parts and kept on with the tearing. A blind man's race. You can just about see but a fingertips reach stepping your path like that. Today's lust is tomorrow's loneliness. The enemy of temptation lurking around every hour as the devouring animal that prowls with no rest. A friend is better than a lover and ultimately one are the same and becomes the other. A pal was hard to come by these days. The main thing they had in common was their abandonment.

He leaves the gate of the fence open and sets his bag in the back seat of his car. Taking out his too old phone he sets it to home and throws it in the passenger seat. It'd be a long stretch of same concrete. He walks out to the middle of the road.

Stepping into a visible beam coming from the moon he feels as though he is under a spotlight. Walls and panels of austere black on every side. He liked to imagine the sounds of the world as that very same world breathing and in such he and his own heart here at the center of the world the peerless heartbeat of it all.

The distance only brought about withdrawn longing tightening the tension of his worries. He felt like he needed to babysit her like a kid who would choke on her own self. She didn't know what to do with herself when she was given the time and they were not having any fun. All to the soundtrack of siren song. Peace and joy an impossibility.

She was a person trying to be a person who realized the effect of the means were not worth the effort of the cause. The way he could read her agitated Eudora. The way she him and in such how he did not know how to shield these robberies of self only those closest to us can hack inside.

It wore her out. It showed on her like a shirt worn too long and stretched too thin. Pitched to him on the day they met was a firm belief that their generation would be the one to save the world. Said it to him over coffee. He took it as the word of God.

They kept the five-dollar bill. Eudora tried to pay. She knew early money was hard on him. Passed that bill on to each the other in secret from then on. The five was gone now. Spent when things got real bad. Got himself a couple shooters.

Lonesome dark where over the hills lay only a penumbra of more night. He tries to picture his life here but cannot. The moonlight has shifted more toward the house and Trasc follows. Gets into his vehicle and starts it. All struggle and no muscle. The only thing American about it was the poverty inside. He writes her a letter. Backs out of the driveway.

When he rights the car and shifts it into drive Eudora runs out the front door of the house. She nearly trips and falls over a box and it is kicked and dragged out with her. Trasc puts the car in park and opens the door and gets out and their bones collide. They breathe their life into one another and drown in each other's shadow. He scoops her into his arms and holds her tight. He can feel her tears on his cheek. His neck.

"Please just come," she says.

"I know."

"I'm sorry. I don't know what's wrong with me. I try and love you how I know I love you."

"It's me."

"No... no..."

"It's me. It's always me."

He sets her bare feet down lightly on the pavement. She cries into his chest.

"We talked about traveling the world together. And all we got..."

High wind. Empty boxes blowing from the side of the house. Eudora kicks one brushing against her ankle. Trasc regards it. Knows the shape of her leg. The length and the taste. The look and the feel to it. If she were sweating in this cold heat he would know the run of that river along that track. Her eyes shift and trace the dimensions of the exterior of their home. Her hands shake. Every time he'd ever made her feel this way and their eyes met he thought about killing himself. She licks the salt on her lips. A light hail patterns about them like birdshot softly drumming these concaves.

"We talked about traveling the world together and all we got put in are boxes."

"We have a lot to be excited for."

"I am. I am excited about our future."

"Me too. Go inside. It's cold."

"Please come."

"I will."

"We'll get a truck and do it together. Make a day out of it. I'll take off. We'll sneak out of that place. Start over. Bandits.

On the run. Look out. Pew pew," she makes finger guns and blows figurative smoke and he laughs.

"Sounds like a plan."

"Remember when we... when you... dined and dashed. I was compliant by association."

"Guilty by association. That's on me. You stole my heart is what you did."

"You sap. Remember the ransack little diner. Kind of cute. The guy working the counter taking his job too seriously. Chasing us down."

"I remember. I remember you as our driver."

"I was on the fly."

"Checking the rearview. Five and ten or whatever the hell on the steering wheel. La-di-da."

"I was playing it cool."

"There's never been playing it safe with you."

"We were lucky."

"Always been."

"Can't run from me."

"Just fast enough to make it all stop spinning."

"People I work with are getting together. I like them. Ro is a cunt but..."

"Damn."

"I know. I'm sorry. Interesting bunch. You can meet my boss. I hope you can make it. You'll like it. My treat."

"Doesn't need to be."

"We should be together."

"I know. I kept you up late. I'm sorry. Go to bed. Call me in the morning."

"Will you sleep?"

"I'll be up."

"Don't drink."

"I won't."

"I love you."

"I love you more."

"It just seems so insignificant."

"What?"

"Everything."

"It does not need to be significant. It just needs to be enough. It is enough."

"I love you."

"Go," he pats her ass. "I left the shotgun."

"Cruiser?"

"Yes."

When Eudora turns to leave something changes in her face. It is sudden and cold. She had sensitive skin. Her moods would show on her flesh. In all its telling her expressions lay barren on her own face. When she kisses him it feels like a dead fly landing on him. The wind feels oppressive. She watches him the whole way. Her eyes glazed over seduced by drug mainlining malice through those gateways. She doesn't look back to him. Just keeps walking on. He loses her in the dark. She'd managed to get a letter on his dash.

To my love. Never give up.

He smiles to that reluctantly. Shakes his head and his smile recedes away to pain. It starts to rain and he wipes away the beads across the glass. Thinks about the windshield wipers scraping away his face. He grips the wheel and slams it once with the note balled inside of it. Tempers his rage.

"Control your reactions," Trasc says. He rights his breathing. Backs out and moves on.

The roads are narrow. Street signs, lights, all life lost. He drives at a rolling pace.

"CALCULATING. RE-CALCULATING."

Heading the wrong way. Backing into a driveway and turning around and on to another way. He nearly hits two cars parked in the cluster.

"CALCULATING. RE-CALCULATING."

The phone won't connect. He stops in the middle of the road and turns his phone off and turns it back on to set up the route. He follows the way amongst the trails orchestrated by the robotic voice. Drives into a dead end. Turns the car around and drives on.

"RE-CALCULATING. CALCULATING. RE-CAL…"

Incommodious floods his being. A street tapered in the middle and all sides and every which way all the way in this thoroughfare web. A coyote in the headlights then it is gone.

He'd been told many things. The Suburban Jungle some striking cops he'd see drinking at the bar would call it. The animal life to be weary of. The summer traffic and the roads. The schools and the drugs. Stories of tragedy and suspect histories became mere subtleties in a place like this.

One of them laughed at him when he said he might be moving up that way. Told him be careful. Don't get lost. Knew he didn't mean just in a direction. Trasc asked him to step outside. Could do that. They weren't on the clock. None of them were. He just wanted to compensate for his self-mortification.

Reversing and then driving and then reversing and driving. Park. Reverse. Drive. Park. Reverse. Drive. He cannot get the car right any which way. Each inch takes him into another car. On a person's lawn. Right up on somebody's house at one o'clock in the morning. He turns off the heat. Turning the wheel and turning it again.

"CALCULATING. RE-CALCULATING."

Churning this gyre until the rear tires dip and the front elevates eyelevel with the dashboard. Trasc goes for a ride upward bound and bound to his vehicle. The car dips backwards into a ditch between sidewalks. He cuts the wheel and revs the pedal to the floor getting all four tires on the road and screams. He smashes his fists on the wheel.

How attractive. The enraged, yelling, lonely, tragic man. Give me a break. It's the desperate masquerading as enlightened these days.

He screams some more. He doesn't allow himself to call Eudora. There would be small forebodings such as these presenting to him the hopelessness of existence without her. The smallest of things became the steepest of triumphs. Trasc blissfully paid five hundred dollars in tickets putting off car legislation with only four hundred in the bank. If it weren't for Eudora his taxes would never get done. He never figured out so young the illusory state of being ponderous and afraid.

He drives the whole way in silence. Hour and a half on the mile. He'll make it all wheels considering in one and change.

He's been here before. This toiling. He considered it all one long weekend. Sometimes they felt heavy to get by but he did. He knew how heedless he was. It was in his blood. He does what it is that there is nothing else but to do. There is a road that he finds that will be his salvation. One last stop along the way.

THREE

The house is twenty minutes from his and Eudora's rental. He came out into the light like extraterrestrial terrain. Tires grinding on the driveway. A light on in the garage. He steps out and walks off to the side door and steps in. A motorcycle parked near storage units in what is a pretty decent sized space. Two sections are divided by homemade counter. Left is a smaller nook where a dart board is set up. Fishing poles line the ceiling. As much raw materials this way and up in the attic to raise a farm.

"Heard your car. What do you want," Rich says.

"How many you have so far?"

"I'm dehydrated."

"Look. I'm sorry."

"Yeah."

"When I come back will you work on the house with me? Show me some things?"

"Still got the apartment?"

"Feel like I got nothing. Don't own anything."

"You're coming up?"

"Rich. I wouldn't do that to Eudora."

"Why aren't you here?" Rich finishes his can and tosses it into a plastic barrel. Cracks open another and takes a long hard pull and snaps back looking straight into Trasc's eyes with two wet drunken ones of his own blue and wild and old as stone, astonished by the nature of his being.

"Y'all fooled me."

"Yeah."

"Thought you let me in."

"We did," he's drunk. Just keeps saying yeah. Slurring his words and rocking in his stool. He throws darts. "Why did you say that."

"What?"

"What would we do if Eudora was gone. Why did you say that?"

"Goodnight, Rich."

He waits for the old man to go inside and circles back and gets what he needs and hits the road home.

FOUR

Driving through a wintery petrichor with his collar turned up into the wind of a cracked window hitting a joint as he drives. Nothing but abandoned shopping centers on the way out of town. Some of the hills felt like he'd been driving off the face of the earth. No place to buy food other than QuickCheks. The foliage overgrown and seemingly roofing the place. A liquor store every fifty yards. Broken down gas stations seem to be the only infrastructure. There's a languor to the place. A sag in every direction.

Something wild sifting in the fragrance. Memories of good spirits pinned behind. He feels enveloped in the cold dry spell of gray skies and the chemicals clung to rusted highway glittering. Racing down twin refineries cascading like giant train tracks that run into a sky littered only by a mirage of clouds. The colors of the smoke and the yellow lights made Trasc feel like it was an attack of some kind.

It was a poignant rejection. A silent car wreck with a tension that can choke. What they had in their time of passage was not a knowledge of self or a better understanding of love but rather a fleeting collection of pretenses, consternations, and boredoms.

I-80. Hard to stay awake. Close your eyes and swerve on out into the abyss and all that blackness. Sink right into the ocean. Wash away this unmendable fatigue. As many times his heart had broken it peeled back layers of the world in which he constructed his own demise. There on his back was the devil and inside of his chest tiny little gods that were merely there to exercise endless crucifixions. Henceforth a prying of his own eyes never to unsee his own end repeating. A constant digging to new realms of rock bottoms.

He'd wonder what the world might look like through a lens of red anvil eyes and just what. Ten years from now. Five. It wasn't just alarmism anymore. Everybody had just about a feeling in the air something is coming down the pike. People had said it to him in routine passing over and over again. Some of them smiled when they said it. The big one is coming. There's an atmospherically apocalyptic unified dread. The social climate dwindling. The night was clearer to him than the blistering day. The tires on the road feel as his legs churning. He wants the heat. Wants the speed.

Past another mile marker. Nobody on the road. Speed sign reading sixty-five. Rising, rising, rising. The old boy traveling the concrete canvas at ninety-five. One hundred. One ten. The steering wheel throttles in his hands. He's got a good way on this road until exit fifty-two toward the Garden State Parkway. Nothing the way of a landmark to replenish his recollection of his whereabouts.

He calls Ford on the mobile. Gets his voicemail. The man left it so as a contact if contacted basis. He hasn't heard from him. Meet and greet is tomorrow. He always regretted committing to things.

"Ford. It's Trasc. Sorry to call so late. Hope it doesn't disturb you. I wanted to check in for tomorrow. Pretty jazzed up about the whole thing. Nerves dragging and kicking and screaming in the chest, you know? Thanks for the opportunity. I always thought there were so many boundaries I couldn't hurdle all things considering getting in this field. I won't let you down. I think I can bring a lot to the scene."

He'd wondered how many times he'd uttered these fatal words. Tell a man what you're worth and you tell him just the merit of that stock. People buy in and put the chips to ride on the value you present to them. He knew Ford to think little of him.

Working nights at the hotel you meet all types of people. The uniform of Trasc's own skin began feeling the fire of the clocking bureaucratic riddles. Meaningless jobs with no monetary gain or self-respect.

Trasc believed you can work it three ways. Work a job that you can stomach aligning with a passion or a hobby of yours. A job if you are lucky enough to get paid to do what you love. Or something where you can help somebody and make a little bit of a difference in the world. You aren't going to change it. But you can help. Help was change and holding the door open was saving the world. Show him a hero and it was somebody who knew how to laugh. In general and at themselves. He was laughing but he was no hero. He felt he hadn't worked a day in his life always working.

Every other day somebody was overdosing or getting shot or stabbed at the hotel. Somebody lost or something stolen. A domestic situation however undomesticated things seemed to be. Evictions. Ford had come in one night working a case. Trasc knew the guy he was looking for. Didn't tell Ford. Looking back at it he knows that Ford found the guy anyway and knew Trasc lied to him.

Ford was probably working him a bit but the two had started talking and Ford started asking questions. Didn't much like Trasc's life situations and employment status.

Folding ragged laundry until the sun came up. Respected that he was a writer. And just like that Trasc was on his way at being a private investigator. There were times where he'd come to believe that Eudora rejected his good fortune.

Trasc pulls over to the side of the road and steps out and moves toward the rear passenger seat with his keys laced between his knuckles. No headlights on the road. The streetlights and the city lights and the stars, the immensity of it all floods into him with meteor force. His determination undermines the cold. He premediated this. Worked himself up to the state. They were right where he left them taking them from Rich. Made sure they wouldn't roll from side to side. Stayed cold. He lines up three cans of Keystone Light on the top of the car and shotguns each one of them.

Lights approaching. Slowing down and peeling off behind him. He can't help but imagine how small and weak he looks. No cops on the road. Some floaters trying their idle hands at noble deeds getting themselves into all sorts of trouble. The car doesn't have that cop austere. Out walks a small classical looking woman in a cloche.

"Are you okay?" she says.

"What?"

"Are you okay?"

"Is that why you stopped? See if I'm okay."

"Yes. Of course."

A stone in his throat. Eyes watering not just from being ethanol loaded. He shakes his head.

"Alright. Heading up 33?"

"I am."

"Two people bleeding out in the road that way. Road rage shooting. Suppose that's what happens now. Some folks got a hundred miles squared away."

"Thanks."

They regard one another a moment. She turns around

and gets back in her car and drives off. Trasc takes the cans and hurls them. A clocking in to be had. He was cleansed and ready to go. A lot of catching up to do. Some days he would think of himself as a fulltime drinker. Committed to the trade. Drink himself into a coma and clemency sleep until six the next night and wake up only to break a sweat so that he can replenish those fluids all over again. It was a dangerous road he knew. The stomach pains and the migraines. Nobody was veering off the side of that road to stop him.

Continuing on NJ-33 on to about the second exit the way he'd come. Driving through sleeping towns such as Asbury where the pallet dances at the culture and the food in the sleeping buildings. Behind locked doors and closed signs it has more life than where he's been. He thinks about sitting over a bar pie cooked thin and well done margherita style with spiced sausages and a beet and goat cheese salad while thinking about his world with the hum of human life around him. From there on with that first good thought he's had all day at this witching hour it was smooth sailing on his way back home.

All the same distances giving way to similar silences. He would think he was the last man on earth. Could go on and live your life not knowing anybody or ever leaving the tiny space he occupied hidden and tucked away in these personal universes. Pulling off into his backend spot in the complex he parks his car and walks up the stairs to the empty apartment feeling like he's dragging around a carcass.

They moved everything out. Next to the single chair and lamp and a stack of books a sheet and pillow are spread across the carpet. A shoe box overflowing with her letters. Her new one in his back pocket. The bottle awaits him very much his lone visitant.

To you.

You gorgeous, lovely man. Did the envelope scare you a little? When you read this hopefully you'll be home. I miss you. I miss sleeping in with you. There's nothing in this world I care about more than I do you. The feeling I get when you step into our home. The love and comfort I feel running into your arms.

You said that I focus only on the bad that you do. But to be completely honest I have no idea what that even means. You are the epitome of the perfect man. The passion and love we have for one another can never go unnoticed. It can't be denied or waved off. I have nothing but respect and admiration for you. You've been given nothing but letdowns and frustrations. To have to watch the person you so deeply love and care for go through that. To not have control over it. It makes me want to breathe fire. My heart can take no more of it.

I will never, could never, give up on you or us. On days when you're feeling like miracles don't exist remember to take a breath and remember that we are on a ball floating in space of infinite nothingness and that ball spins mightily slowly. Remember I left and came back. And that allows us to be in this life with each other.

Adonis. You are a miracle to me. Your passion and your intellect. Your mind and soul. Your body. Mhm. Your body. Thank you for all that you do for me. For the love and care you've shown me. For the words of encouragement. The push to always shoot for more.

I appreciate you. No matter where life takes us we will always be on top of the world. It's our world. I need you to know how proud I am of you. How incredibly strong I know you to be. You are a hero, my hero, and you give me strength and purpose.

The pain and devastation you must feel is probably tearing you up inside. Difficult to fill up. I know. I don't blame or fault you for anything. Our love will grow deeper and stronger in this.

You deserve nothing but the best. You deserve peace and happiness and to lay your head down every night knowing we have the love of a lifetime. You are forever a part of me. Of my life and my family. You have people who care about you. On your darkest days I hope to be your light guiding you out. Comforting you. Loving. Peace.

You need to understand that I deeply care for you. If I were to ever lose you a huge chunk of me would be lost.

I need you to take better care of yourself. You should be sleeping more and drinking less. If you ever feel as though no one cares, say that to my face and see what happens. I'd fight you. Fight for you. I'll always root for you. I will always be the voice in your ear bringing you back to me.

You have a home in me. A friend. Confidant. Lover. You have me. There is such a loneliness out there.

Come home. I can tell you I'm waiting. Desperately need your touch. Your presence. I know you're afraid. You don't have to be. We have each other. Please be careful. Being good to you is being good to me. I haven't written one of these in a long time and I'm sorry for that. I am sorry about a lot of things. Lately it's been hard. Lately it's been harder...

Signing off. She could save him. She'd done so. But he could not save her. He brings the letter to his lips.

"Ah, darlin."

The wetness from his eyes blots the ink. Talking to herself. She wrote notes when she was a kid. Suicide letters to her family and best friend. To think like that as a child. She was that self-aware. She was that smart. It wasn't a thinking with her but rather a wisdom. He knew how that doesn't go away. She wasn't doing it for anybody but herself.

Eudora pulled him out of such shallows. Always his earth angel, his Virgil. He'd muddled and confused things in the murk to get a quick fix of this front he'd been putting up his whole life. All she'd ever given him was beauty, joy, patience, kindness, and love. Compassion, understanding, and faithfulness.

He opens the box and begins to read other letters but can't bring himself to go on. Didn't like that even in being it felt as though he should be in mourning. He wanted to hold her tight and toss her hair and taste her tongue.

Trasc drinks himself to sleep to numb away the pain. It doubles down on the hurt and he chases it with the very means of an end to this long night. To go about dealing with his failure with compassion. He felt hellbent to aimlessly wander his tragic self, never undermining the spectacle found in this trauma.

He didn't bother to get his bag or his phone from the car. He had everything that he needed. He was alone and everything was fine.

THE PEOPLE OF THE STATE OF NEW JERSEY,
PLAINTIFF,
-VS-   CASE NO. ███████
███████ DEFENDANT

REPORTER'S TRANSCRIPT OF PROCEEDINGS
MARCH 10, 2033

APPEARANCES:

FOR THE PEOPLE: ███████
                                  DEPUTY DISTRICT ATTORNEY

FOR THE DEFENDANT: N/A

OFFICIAL COURT REPORTER: ███████
                                  C.S.R. NO. 10907

HOPATCONG, NEW JERSEY: MARCH 10, 2033

PROCEEDINGS (9 OF 27)

THE COURT: Mr. Trasc. No matter the verdict of this case in these proceedings on the events that occurred on JANUARY 15TH, 2023, I wanted to say that the court appreciates your participation in here today.

MR. TRASC: You say that like I had a choice.

THE COURT: You did.

MR. TRASC: Not how it felt when your dogs came sniffing around my property.

THE COURT: I heard it was quite secluded.

MR. TRASC: It is. Privacy has gone up in smoke with the last good book writ and the last good song, too. Both came out a long time ago. They don't try with the movies anymore. The golden TV thing ended right quick. What I'm saying is away ain't a concept other than the things we love slipping away. It's not a place or a direction to aim to. It isn't real. No place and no thing and there's no way of getting to it. Best make peace with the here and now wherever that is wherever you may be and whatever it is you might have done. Nobody gets away and everybody is guilty. Something tells me we'll reach that destination everyone together all at once making love to the sky. Find that away was only ever to never have been. Nonexistence is not a place to be. It is the place to stay. Here I am getting work done out in the yard and your boys roll up digging old graves. Wait. Hold up. Don't quote me on that. I'm sorry. There was a girl. A lady cop. Very unsentimental of me. This is national right? Eyes on this. Don't want the wolves set against me. Lock me up for that alone. Diversity and equality and feminism I'm like yeah sick brother. Right on. You want to tell me what this is all about? Second time now and I'm still in the dark. This doesn't look like a court. Don't feel like a court.

THE COURT: You are using crass language. I would advise you to tread lightly. You might incriminate yourself.

MR. TRASC: I thought I was here voluntarily.

THE COURT: Be as direct as possible. We are not looking to be enlightened.

MR. TRASC: Only entertained. I'm not looking to be profound. Gave up being the mistaken prophet and instead gave way to being the misunderstood priest. Everything has lost its meaning and everything is known. Just waiting on calamity. Everything has been said and the only thing left is the silence that no longer has definition and too carries destruction in its wake and booms inside my head. Everything feels artificial and has no flavor as we suck on machines. We have strayed too far from God and the drift will continue. There is no stopping it. Our collective forsakenness exasperated a jump start. I tell myself this is why all the writers are dead. They couldn't see through this funhouse smoke show hall of mirrors. Lot of cameras and people out there for us to tell the same story. I can barely remember what happened. Remember much of anything. Saw that getting difficult for people. Remembering shit. Thinking. The Great Depression but not in the way you usually mean it. The Great Brain Drain. The Big Poisoning. Drugged and drank and scrolled away some circuits up there myself. Some stories you don't want to be told but we hear them. Force fed I suppose. World's voice too loud to ignore. That pale horse was kicking. Kicking us from the inside. Our spirits–and I don't mean in any pious sense– seem to be in great peril. This is a time to be brave. To have faith in our hearts. And I'm afraid there's a shortage of that. Looking to the stars and looking inside yourself aren't opposites. Just in different directions. Seems as though what we got ourselves into. What we're into now. What's inside. There wasn't much to find in there. In that lonely room.

THE COURT: Just tell it straight.

MR. TRASC: I had a point to make but forgot it. Stopped trying to prove them a long time ago. Wise man told me not to argue with fools. Stopped talking to myself in that regard, too.

THE COURT: You need to take this seriously.

MR. TRASC: Sorry.

THE COURT: It's alright.

MR. TRASC: I'm not here to prove my innocence.

THE COURT: No.

MR. TRASC: Because you caught who killed those two kids.

THE COURT: Correct.

MR. TRASC: Ten years ago.

THE COURT: Yes.

MR. TRASC: But there's been some new revelations.

THE COURT: That's right.

MR. TRASC: There we have it. Loose ends tied off at the end. All anybody keeps saying these days. This world is going to hell in a handbasket. Shit. Reject that. Even if the thought of any future is starry-eyed and the past is of false memory bringing to bear real-world travesties in our present moment of madness and mania tangible the way static is. I say instead world and all of us are going to heaven in a little itty-bitty canoe. Keep telling myself this'll be the year we move closer into the light. Just not the sort of one that snuffs out all the rest.

THE COURT: Can you state exactly what you see? For the record.

MR. TRASC: You. Me. Person scribbling in the corner over there. A camera. And this guy. Who the hell is this guy?

THE COURT: Mr. Trasc.

MR. TRASC: Right. It's just that this place is pretty fucking depressing. And he looks uncomfortable. Seriously. Who is he? Where's the jury? Members of the public?

THE COURT: Last time.

MR. TRASC: I'm just saying. I saw some great signs out there. We can hang them up or...

THE COURT: We are done.

MR. TRASC: Come on. We are here in the name of truth. You'd turn your back on justice? How dare you.

THE COURT: You won't make a mockery of this.

MR. TRASC: You already did that. Locked up the wrong person. Talking to people already that I haven't seen in years without us corresponding with one another. Trading our information or reciting our past truths. Tossed away the key on a poor innocent soul all this time. Add to that this sketch ass operation you got going on here.

THE COURT: I am warning you.

MR. TRASC: It's just that. Look. I'm a little high.

THE COURT: Goodbye, Mr. Trasc. We will reschedule.

MR. TRASC: Hold on just a minute. It's medical. Damn near sell these things out of ice cream trucks nowadays. Besides, I am here on an admissible basis. I thank God for it. Being sober. I should be dead or drunk. Never thought I would see these years. The valleys leading to this place and the petty qualms within it.

THE COURT: This is a lot steeper than squalor. You know this. You have to know this. We will not make light of the dead here, Mr. Trasc.

MR. TRASC: I have no intention of doing that. Not a day goes by that I don't look up and say thank you the moment my feet touch the ground. No man has been more blessed or lucky than I have been. My life is a story worth telling and it is God or a higher power who is the star of it. Been trying to find deeds to my faith a long time now. Being in here reminds me of Achilles and Odysseus making their peace in the underworld. My expiation has expired.

THE COURT: Do you feel as though you have something you might want to confess?

MR. TRASC: You bet.

THE COURT: Tread lightly.

MR. TRASC: You asked.

THE COURT: Your surroundings.

MR. TRASC: You. Me. Some dude sitting over there staring at the wall. Buddy. Ease up. We are all here for the greater good. Hell of a job. Keep it up. Great form. Stoicism the new black. What's he supposed to be?

THE COURT: Continue.

MR. TRASC: A lady typing away in the corner. A camera positioned in front of me. There's a roof to these four symmetrical walls and a lone door behind you with a panel of glass next to it that I can't see out. And the walls. I don't know. I can't really say white. Not yellow. Kind of like an enchanted ginger. No. Hot khaki. I'm sorry. I used to know somebody who wanted to name a color. Was on her bucket list.

THE COURT: Can you state your name.

MR. TRASC: Adonis Trasc.

THE COURT: Age.

MR. TRASC: Thirty-nine.

THE COURT: Why are you here. Straight. In your own words.

MR. TRASC: My own words.

THE COURT: Yes.

MR. TRASC: Exhaustion. I look back on it now and I think that's pretty much the angle on things. We were pretty exhausted from the jump. You look back on your life and there is a cycle of endless build ups and let downs. Makes you bone tired. I remember all of us taking that undertaking like some kind of oath. I don't know. It was a diverse lot. But we were all pretty mashed to bits. Saw too much love lost. Worked hard with nothing working. It's exhausting. It didn't matter for any of us. Our calluses aligned. It was like it was waiting on us. This bad trouble. Bad decision addictions. Too many mistakes. Just sort of beat up emotionally. Bored and unsatisfied out of our minds. Melancholia is what they used to call it.

THE COURT: You said you were a writer.

MR. TRASC: Always hated that question. What do you do. I do a lot of things. People don't care. Don't listen. Want to know only in order to judge. Shouldn't give much worth to that.

THE COURT: What do you write?

MR. TRASC: Fiction. The majority of us really went there to work at something. It's tragic. It's terrible. You seen it. We had a lot of broken hearts breaking bread breaking some heads and everything between. We caused some mayhem.

THE COURT: They said you were building something. The people who took you in.

MR. TRASC: A boat. Euroclydon. Never was much of a handyman. Who has time for new tricks, you know? I feel like it's owed to people.

THE COURT: Owed?

MR. TRASC: Don't question my faith and I won't question your theory.

THE COURT: Are you planning a trip?

MR. TRASC: I'm planning for the end. No hard feelings.

THE COURT: Not many people know you.

MR. TRASC: What?

THE COURT: I said that not many people know who you are.

MR. TRASC: Who knows anybody, right?

THE COURT: We know there were six of you.

MR. TRASC: Who's funding this?

THE COURT: On record we have your statements on Eudora's whereabouts.

MR. TRASC: I didn't know there was a record.

THE COURT: She's dead.

MR. TRASC: She's not dead. She's gone.

THE COURT: Okay. You mentioned a bucket list. What else was on it?

MR. TRASC: I'm sorry?

THE COURT: You knew somebody who wanted to name a color. They had a bucket list. What other things were on it?

MR. TRASC: I don't remember.

THE COURT: Did they name the color?

MR. TRASC: No. No they didn't.

THE COURT: The man you were operating with. Who was he?

MR. TRASC: Operating is your way of putting it.

THE COURT: Yes. You were hunting for what our records show to be a suspect known here only as The Boxman. Different killings. Another case.

MR. TRASC: Another case and another case and on and on and on. Seems dramatic.

THE COURT: It was.

<AMENDMENT>

WHAT FOLLOWS IS A TRANSCRIPTION IN LIVE EVENT OF THE PROCEEDINGS. THE TRANSCRIPTION WAS HANDWRITTEN.

"Door to the room opens. No sound of struggle outside. A man with a gun. Raises up. Shouting. 'THE HOUR OF TRIAL IS TO COME ON THE WHOLE WORLD TO TEST THE INHABITANTS. THE HOUR OF TRIAL OF THE EARTH. DESTRUCTION HAS NOT BEEN SLEEPING. MAN WAS BORN TO HEAVEN AS SPARKS RISE TO HEAVEN.' The man shoots the Plaintiff and himself. People flood the room with phones."

PART 2

FIVE

2007

They called it the Circle. When you turned off and into the development that's what it was, Lotus Lane, a circle. Stretch the Circle out and it might be the length of a few football fields. Coil back up like a snake.

It was the only turn off a road that stretched for about twenty miles that opened up and peeled off out into fields of suburbia blooming in multiple seams. Lotus Lane was about three turns in. Houses stood like caricatures. Most of them abandoned.

Across the main road a church was being built. The kids sit outside the Circle in the church without roof making a chlorine bomb. Seven in sum. Breaking up the little tablets into small pieces and sticking them into the stripped soda bottle. Later investigations would pin them inside here. People working on the church catching scent of swimming pools. The two brothers from Ohio do the chemistry. The bigger one likes to fight. Says he's a boxer. Is a little strange. Kind of slow and unpredictable.

The other doesn't say much. Gauges and sleeves and piercings. Skinny jeans and chemically straightened hair.

He's kind of disinterested in the whole thing and finishes and skates off. At night the group descends into the Circle.

They walked around it a few times. They were recording the big one from Ohio, Tom, on flip phones. He's on about endless ramblings as somebody gone completely insane. Word of the boys from Ohio losing their mother there. Said she was murdered. The killer never found. Left her on the front lawn of the house.

They live the first turn in, furthest out from the Circle. Nobody knows or ever sees the father. They have another brother with his head on right. A part of the wrestling team. The other has his crowd and his scene. Nobody ever sees much of Tom around school.

They come up on them just a few months back moving into the block. The other boys have been friends their whole lives. They settle on a house a quarter of the way around the circle. The plainest and most somber looking. No amenities and nothing much going on save for the initial blueprint. The pulse of life coming from inside. Pale blue light and chatter of a television. The house has a bright pink door that is open to a glass one.

They stand on ceremony when they do it, usually sticking the bomb inside of mailboxes. They needed to draw sticks because of the fear of blowing your hand up when you shook the thing to activate it and place it inside.

Tom steps up in the choosing over the huddling boys. Takes the chlorine bomb and runs up to the door and opens it. He shakes the bomb and tosses it inside. Most of the boys remember that frozen moment and the look on Tom's face. They remember a mother screaming who cannot save her child. It was the last time anybody ever saw Tom or the kids from Ohio.

SIX

PRESENT TIME

Being here for almost twenty years Daniella still cannot stand not being able to walk a few blocks down a life riddled road or across a bridge and choose a new spot to get a bite to eat in the morning. To read with coffee from a French café. The closest hotspot was a fifteen-minute drive up toward a Starbucks right next to a Target across the street from a Walmart. This side of Jersey had last offices culture.

A piece of her would long for bits of New York. Staten Island or Brooklyn where they spent most of their time. Certain elements and textures of the place. All the rhythms and the hums of the area. All these years and John would still laugh at the sounds of the city alarm she'd wake herself up to. She'd come to appreciate the silence of the neighborhood. It took some time to come around to it. No sounds of kids or play out there in the street. She wondered how a day can be so bright and so lifeless.

Cold water to the face. She keeps the water running and plugs the drain. John was still sleeping. She can hear Malachi in the kitchen. She's laughing, probably listening to a podcast. She kept trying to get her to switch over to audiobooks. Thought of those things as podcasts before podcasts were podcasts. They would just piss John off.

"Everybody has got something to say. Like people should hear it. Fuck out of here. Spare me the vanity. Who or what qualifies them for this? I feel dumber listening. Got one of these for everything. How much of this crap is out there? Here's my podcast. Called sit down and shut your mouth. Sitting inside and listening to people talk instead of going to talk to the people. Vaffanculo."

Like a bad start to a novel she looks at herself square in the face in the mirror. She never understood why that was considered so. The act took gumption. To look yourself square in the eyes and hold that gaze. She raised Malachi to each morning make it a routine. Five minutes look yourself in the eye and make peace. If you cannot hold your own how are you to hold others? They would do it together. Somewhere along the way they stopped.

We do not hold hands. We lock eyes. A firm grip is no held gaze. Don't take ones who don't like you looking.

She'd taken to reading to pass the time. She still didn't have the best grasp on the language and allowed herself to get lazy. Made a sort of application for herself. Treated the reading like a job and like the first rule of any job it was in her just to show up. She chose difficult texts. Tomes to shorter works. Read all day down to just a few second bursts. John had his residential enterprise but to her the days were becoming harder to fill. She too feared this for Malachi.

The water runs into the sink. Daniella looks all the harder, searching for things to not like in her appearance. The mirror reflected other aesthetics. Shortcomings as a mother, a lover, a friend. As an entrepreneur and in her faith.

Malachi is on the phone. She can hear John stirring awake. He's saying his morning prayers over the memorial he keeps in the room. This would be hers. Matrimony to these unrelinquished satisfactions and binding losses.

The water in the sink runs over the edges and Daniella turns it off. She turns the shower on and opens the lone window. Turns and listens outside the bathroom door to the sounds of her life. She dips her face into the water and screams. Comes up gasping controlling the volume of her own breathing. Submerges herself once more and screams again. Her own percolating soul bubbles in her face when John knocks on the door. She pats her face dry and practices a smile and opens the door and it seems to work on him.

"Morning, baby," John says.

He's holding coffee and she takes it and sips it and kisses him on the mouth. His lips are warmer than what is inside the cup. A chalice even after all these years. Her man and she his woman. Together with fractures and all this is their kingdom.

"Hey."

"What's wrong?"

"Nothing."

"Dani," he moves the hair back behind her ears. Traces the tattoo down her side. Picks her up and places her on the countertop. Buries his face into her hips. It is everything in her to mask her screaming again. She can smell herself on his breath. "Talk to me, baby."

"I'm getting old."

"Tastes new to me. Try something new down there?"

"Take me seriously."

"I pray at the altar of you."

"You pray at her feet."

"Baby, I know. It was just a way of putting things."

"How is she?"

"Good, baby. She's real good."

"Did she speak to you today?"

"She did."

"What'd she say?"

"Said there was this bald spot in the back of my head…"

Daniella pushes him into the wall. Even at his age it still feels like hitting brick. The way it did all those years ago when her heart was racing and he took her shirt off for the first time and she his.

None of the boys would talk to her. Men these days talk much about men of old but it is only a façade. A fever dream and a wish. Time and pain warped and twisted these memories of reverie. Conducted these stories to better fit present timeframes in the way of mainlining nostalgic images that fester from the creativity of those looking. Daniella came to this country from another country and knew that men were few and far between. Men like her father. Men she loved and respected. Noble and decent men who were honest and of sound tenderness and honorability. The confidence John had when he walked up to her was something beyond their years. Looked her right in the eyes. Destined doomed fateful lovers.

"We get old too quick but I'm chasing you the whole nine, divine," John says.

"You're aging like the grapes you have growing up the side of the house. I look terrible."

"Not the way I see it."

"How so."

"I'm a stay-at-home dad."

"You're not a stay-at-home dad."

"You have the restaurant. What a fine eatery it is. People are talking about it."

"People can't go to it."

"This too shall come to pass."

"So says the Reaper."

John puts a finger over her mouth.

"He's not that anymore."

"What then?"

"Father. Husband. Artist. Businessman. Probably in that order. Sorry, baby."

"It's okay. She's off to college now. First label softly glides away. You'll only be mine. They spend more time with the world than they do with us. My mother used to tell me that we are all children of the light. That there's a star with our name on it and that is where we go when we die. That we borrow one another's blaze. Cradled inside all that white fire. Borrowed light, like the moon and the sun. That constellations are just the shapes of our souls. A community in the heavens. Families put back together. Our babies are stars, John."

A beat between them. John thinks about her words.

"I'm sorry," Daniella says.

"She was a good woman."

"Who?"

"Madreda."

"She was. I loved her. And Mal's here telling me she hates me last night."

"Just a phase. Darkness before the dawn, right?"

"Do you believe what she said? My mother."

"It's not what I believe. It's what I want to believe. What we choose to. Your mother says connect the dots, bring me back to you. I'm like yeah. Okay. It's only ever been lightness with you. Through it all. Through the dark. Baby, I was blind and now I see. If I can have you here, if we can have what we got, who is to second guess a world beyond this world. Something speculative being here. In this love. Who is to say where the light goes. Where love goes when it's all gone. I know your Mama is dancing up there with her. Etching new horizons. Graffiti nebulas twirling in their wake."

She pushes him against the wall. Hadn't realized she'd begun to cry. John trails small pools with his thumb down her cheek.

"What do you say. Freshmen fifteen?" he says.

"More like thirty. All this time off. I'm getting fat."

"I've been meaning to ask you. How do I look in this skin?"

They kiss long and hard.

"Let's fuck it all away. Impossibly beautiful woman."

SEVEN

John sits in his music studio built within the confines of the unfinished basement of the house. Soundproof walls, he doesn't like being in here. Doesn't like not being able to hear things. To smile at just the sounds of Daniella and Malachi being. Knowing who's who just by the pace and force of their movements and their steps. Knowing their silences and their drift.

Get in and get out. He treats everything that he does away from his family as a debt of honor and dutiful responsibilities. All writ in stone with blood. His life changed many times. He hoped the growth shared a distant relation to evolutions. Sound philosophy that one does not lose their mind. They surrender them willingly. You lose your ability to change and become a vehicle for cautionary idleness and stagnation. His life changed exponentially when he started viewing time as currency.

It is a booth of technicolor nature. Translucent and free flowing tranquility. He stands at a makeshift standing desk listening to the tracks from the night before. Adjusts the levels and adds a little reverb and plays with the beat.

Reworks some bars and lays them on the track like the kid hoped that he would. The kid had heart and talent. What he doesn't have is the street. He can't create art in a place like this. In a state of comfort. Something that would be nondisposable. Not in the Circle.

It was this. Then it was graffiti art birthday party for the Whites down at house nine. Needed to deliver some clams down at fifty-six. Some flower to sixty to help with the back pain. He would have to field some visits and calls to collect on some of the summer work he'd been syphering off to the youth of the neighborhood. Finally, it would be filming a motorcycle music video down in the cul-de-sac around the bend right in the heart of the Circle. Come night it'd be wining and dining with Daniella, homecooked by yours truly.

He can't believe these sorts of things are numbered and by such simple regard. He would try and solve the cityscape direction and numerical equations the night before certain jobs in the streets of New York. You needed to know the operations of those sorts of things. Now it was just last one on the left. This number and that number. Yellow curtains, can't miss them. It remained as if he moved coast to coast and not just the next state over.

Finishing touches on one final song. This just about finished him. He could not allow that. Would not be beaten by it. The song was for his daughter. Father of two now one. Hit and run. Never did catch the guy. John couldn't stop hugging the little coffin at the funeral. Wouldn't let them put it in the ground. Started filling the grave back up with his hands. His father dragged him away. Said it was weakness. Slapped him in the face. Told him his mother died all over again.

John had his best guys tearing the city apart for years. One of the reasons Daniella got them out of there. Raise Malachi up right someplace else. He never told her, this woman he vowed to and so took the claim of those vows as code to live by. To break them would be for every vein to burst and bleed out. He would never lie to her save one. Never told her that he thought it was all bullshit.

Hostile world guardian. Teaches them things by showing them what you would never say. Total crap to think that raising up a kid under the same blue sky and over the same green grass someplace else would change the collision course they'd be on with themselves. As if setting instilled character. It didn't matter where you went. There was no place to run from yourself. It embodies and encompasses the same journey.

He'd been working on the song for a few years now. It remains unfinished. He stops it when the piano comes in and puts his face in his hands. He can hear the words in his head but he cannot find them to write down.

"You're on repeat, mi amore. You are always repeating."

———

Daniella is waiting for him at the door when John steps out of the basement.

"Company outside. You're in deep merda this time, John."

"Dammit."

John opens the front door. A trio of girl scouts. Beyond them what presents itself to him is some sort of theme park. Just the way these neighborhoods looked to him.

"Give it to me," he says.

"It ain't looking good."

"Nobody eats cookies anymore? It was the Samoas wasn't it? I knew the name would bring about outrage. Be the end of us."

"We got some high blood pressures. Some diabetes. A

wide range of autoimmune diseases. People cutting back on the sugar.”

“So what. YOLO. Push the product a little harder. What do I pay you for?”

“Some vegans.”

“Asleep at the wheel. Knew I should have gotten in the game. Hey. Seventeen owes. Gave you the I’m good for it good for nothing jive how many times?”

“He lost his job.”

“I don’t care. He owes.”

The girls hand John boxes and envelopes.

“Thank you, ladies. Good work,” John reaches into one of the envelopes and hands the girls cash and they head on down the road. Malachi slips through the crack heading out towards the driveway before he can shut the door. “Hold up.”

She keeps moving.

“Mal.”

She stops at the end of the walkway and turns facing him.

“Where you heading?”

“School.”

“Back in session?”

“That’s right.”

“We at that stage?”

“What stage?”

“Stage where you hate me.”

“I don’t hate you, dad.”

“You tell that to your mother?”

“I’m sorry.”

“You don’t need to go if you don’t want to.”

“I want to.”

“Okay. Listening to that crap again?” John gestures to his ears in mentioning her headphones.

“Yeah. Well. Not the crap you’re thinking. But it’s crap.”

“What is?”

"The hearing. The shooting. It's kind of sick how they televise these things. People getting obsessed. Fighting about it. They're saying the cops across the country are walking off the job on this one. I don't know. I'm kind of sick of it. Not my problem."

"Hey."

"What."

"Don't be talking that way."

"Like what?"

"Like it's no problem of yours. Look around you, Mal. If it's him or hers or anyone's problem, it's your problem. You got that? We're all family."

"Sure hope not."

"Thinking about driving up, up and away soon. Your mama and I. Want to come?"

"Okay."

"Leave the screens behind."

"Okay."

"They'll be talking about it at school. Strong suspicion college grounds like to give their opinions on these sorts of things."

"Not very strong opinions."

"Not so. You don't need to give yours."

"Long breaths of trahison des clercs talking to some of these cats."

"That's my girl. Trahison des clercs. You'll have to break that down for me. Over dinner later. You pray for the dead?"

"Yes."

"Good."

"What good will that do?"

"What's that?"

"Praying."

"You'll have to figure that out yourself."

"Okay."

"People reveal themselves all the time to you. Just pay attention. Stay away from the brutal. Be lyrical, Tesoro. Crossed with poetry. Owe me some lines by the way."

"You owe me some cash."

He hands it to her.

"Consider it an advance. Avoid the herd, Mal."

"Bye, dad."

"I love you."

"I love you, too, dad."

"Listen," Malachi stops and John moves closer. "They'll be feeding you all kinds of lies. School. About this country and the history of this country. The way we as a people should think and be and live. Look around you. Your parents came here and their parents before them. A revolving door. You'll see that the college is ripe full of the diversity they say we so lack. The culture is saturated by it. And girls like you keep giving yourselves away to them."

He grips Malachi's arm too tightly and pulls her closer.

"Dad..."

"Mal. You ever bring a black boy to bed or this house, I'll kill both of you. Think before you speak. You are a beautiful girl. You can't afford to talk stupid."

She pulls away. Looks around horrified. The day bright and clear. Malachi gets into her car and drives away. Every time he watches those plumes rise and distance itself to measures unto faint to him he feels those eyes go the distance and travel a ways over her. He says a silent prayer in his head for her to go safely. For her to return to him.

"You better be careful with that," a man calls over from his yard.

"What's fragile?"

"Your ignorance, dear buddy."

"Morning, Ford."

"John."

Ford tosses files into the back of an unmarked sedan. Places a coffee cup on top of it. Breathes in the air and looks up into the sun and closes his eyes with his face locked on that distant star as if in some form of photosynthesis sucking in all that light.

"What use is there indeed," Ford says.

"What?"

"Praying. You know a translator for silence?"

"Sure do."

"Stopped wasting my breath. Going to need something more than words to stop what's coming. What's walking this earth."

"Faith, hope, and love brother. It's the new black. Think of it as meditation."

"Always a new dark. Reminds me of the nine eleven. Can smell the salt in the air. Taste blood."

A beat between the two men.

"They'll forgive all kinds of things that you do to them," Ford says.

"Women? I know. As long as you give them a good time."

"Jesus, John. Your kid."

"Right."

"When you got one like that. One with a good heart. You'll break it by being a dickhead. Just don't be a dickhead no more, John."

"How's your marriage?"

"Which one?"

"You live alone in that house?"

"That's the one."

"Kids?"

"Not a single one. More of a conscious decision. People don't think those sorts of things through."

"A guy gets too lonely and he gets sick."

"A smarter John said."

"I'll take advice from somebody who has a little more experience in the field."

"I do. I'm older than you. This is a life thing. Man to man. You keep saying shit like that and I'll bust you in the mouth."

"How long we known each other?"

"Too damn long."

"Being a parent is hard."

"No need for tough love. Love is tough enough."

"Love can't be a part of your sales pitch. People want cold hearted these days."

"Those are your days."

"Glory days."

"We both got them."

"When cops could be cops and criminals were actual criminals. Using their hands."

"I never thought of you as a criminal. We both know I'm not copping no more."

"In uniform."

"What do you call this," Ford holds up his tie.

"I call that a noose."

"All your duplicities don't need to be theirs. Only purity. We know you are without a lick of it. It goes away all too soon. You ever think what it's like for her to be out and having herself a day with your bullshit running around her head."

"You going to arrest me?"

"I told you. Not that anymore."

"You're something. What you got going on today? Old timers like us need regimen. Need schedule. Movement is paramount."

"My bones hurt. Can't keep up with the times."

"Bowed out the race a long time ago."

"These things get worse and worse."

"Case by case?"

"Generation by generation."

"You want to talk about it?"

"Nope."

"Boxman?"

"That'd be the one."

"Crazy shit."

"Crazed indeed. These days crazy feels contagious."

"I can get my guys on it."

"My guys didn't get your guys?"

"Not all of them."

"No thanks, John."

"Who hired you?"

"The parents. It's always the parents."

A beat.

"Sorry, John. No offense."

"None took."

"On the canvas of this stage lay a world in unrest. Tent cities in this housing crisis. Food and water shortages. Now a police strike. The flooding. A violent killer on the loose set to prove that love is a mere fabrication and I got not the slightest trace. And here you are with one job to provide some emotional stability and love and you go on and spread more of the problem by spouting out completely insane, racist, hateful, despicable, stupid shit. You make me sick. It's crazy they let you live here."

"You yell at me more than my wife."

"It's what friends are for."

"How long you think they'll be off the job? Saw this one coming. Seems serious this time."

"In for some big changes. It's not my battle."

"I don't know. It seems they're a bit the same. Like these problems are reoccurring and the world just keeps on spinning. Daniella is going a bit stir crazy. Needs something to do."

"Maybe. You like to tell people how they feel. What they need."

"You want some company out there? You need some company."

"Nah."

"Good. Was banking on that."

"Meeting a kid."

"A partner?"

"More like an internship."

"Meaning that there's another one of those things out there."

"That's right."

"Dammit all to hell."

"Seems about the way we're heading."

"Well, cowboy. Rein it in. On your way."

"Keep the neighborhood safe while I'm gone."

"Fuck these people. This place. Bunch of psychopaths. I'm out numbered, Ford."

"Don't do that."

"What?"

"Think you're better than these people."

"Places like this. It grows on you. And not in the good way. Kind of like a tumor."

"It's not that bad."

"It's a circle. A damn toilet bowl."

"And Brooklyn is a maze."

"We keep it that way to keep them out. Be careful out there."

Ford smiles at that and is on his way. Gets into his vehicle listening to a voicemail on his mobile. He hangs up and shuts the door and starts the car. John walks towards his house. Daniella is in the doorway smiling and saying her hello to Ford. John kisses his wife on the head and wraps an arm around her and sees Ford off. Ford backs out of the driveway and rolls down his window.

"Anniversary is coming up, right?"

"Parade's this weekend. We'll drive in together," Daniella says.

"Sure thing. Welp. Date with Satan. Keep on keeping on."

"You'd be surprised where angels might make their way."

Ford taps the horn twice and drives off into the sun. John thinks he sees someone off in the distance looking in on them, feminine in stature. Staring right at Daniella and John in their doorway from out in the middle of the road. He'd watched his only friend be devoured in flame as he drove off. Small black spots in his vision. Tells himself that it's only a trick of the light. All this bucolic wonder. He imagines being flattened across the pavement nothing more than a line of street paint, taking his daughter's place them many years ago. Regurgitating old roads and old ways and new tragedies. Always the hollow and black and cold road it begins it ends and it stays. His whole life there. The road his womb his crib his bed and his coffin.

Just a trick of the light. This flat proliferation of nothingness. A trick of all this light.

EIGHT

Time settles into him dreadful. Waking in a manner of possession. Pain and the memory of pain.

Trasc's head is booming. Empty cans and bottles around him. With that dread comes a knowing. He's late.

"Fuck," he gets up from off the floor, his body screaming, spalled blood flowing throughout him. "FUCKFUCKFUCK."

He looks around for his phone but cannot find it. The barren apartment makes it clear that there is nothing inside but what he can see in a quick study. No water with him. The refrigerator was empty and molded. Anything the way of food would have been what it always was. Whatever he could scrounge out. Cans of sardines. Some hardboiled eggs. He'd go hungry for long stretches. He turns the kitchen faucet on to the droning of pipes. A few spats of brown-yellow water the same color as the rotten light spilling in from fogged windows. He sees his every breath. He can't remember the last thing he paid for. Gas and alcohol were the only things on the budget. You needed to make cuts in modes of being such as these. His stomach ignites.

He should have been right out the door but still he takes

his time. First consistent roof over his head. Worked hard at it his whole life right here before him and lost again. He can feel the weather outside. These chronic annihilating genesis destructions. He takes the place in. Not a memory gone by. His throat and tongue raw. He and Eudora put a lot of love here. Wonders if that would be something future occupants might know and feel.

When he gets out to his car his landlord sits on the hood. She wears a cheap dress and keeps her legs open. When she tosses across a crooked smile on her face it's all tangled and maimed and hard to see because her red lipstick is on her teeth. He didn't think anything of that or her appearance, but it bothered him that she was here and on his car. He parked off the beaten path.

"Morning," she says.

He imagines what he might look like. The sun sits high and small and white. It is a kind of brightness that hurts. Looking any direction feels as though his eyes roll across broken glass. The concrete blasted by cold heat. It hits him like something physical. In a combat sport with the sky.

He feels highlighted. Pressure right up under the inside of his face. He feels puffy and bloated and ravaged with thirst. She's holding a bottle of water and he can't help but stare. Eating a pastry from a gas station. He can almost smell colors. Makes him sick. She chases each bite sucking on a vape. The chill in the air is too much for it to be so blinding.

"What are you doing here?" she says.

"What do you mean?"

"What are you doing here?"

"I live here."

"You're late."

"Have I ever?"

"No."

"No."

"I don't care about that. They don't care about that. They just care about money."

"They know people can't work."

"What are you doing now?"

"Excuse me?"

"Somebody came by looking for you. A woman. Wanted to give you money."

Something in his eyes tells her to move on and he gets in his car. There's water in his bag. Eudora put it there. He drinks the bottle. It could have been completely saturated with the toxins and the plastics and still he would have needed to take it on. Grabs his phone and it's dead so he plugs it in. He knows no way of getting there. It'll take a minute to turn on. He wraps his skull in his hands and screams. Veers out the side window and sees his landlord looking in.

———

Eudora was about three hours into a thirteen-hour shift and didn't answer his call. Ford sent a single text message with a location. It took him to an off handle on the parkway. Trasc almost turned around on the whole thing only there wasn't anywhere to turn and he'd already pulled over. Put his hazard lights on, got out, and locked the door. The day had darkened. Ashy baby blue moved like currents in the all-around in a way that had Trasc stop and gaze at the road and all the passing lights.

There was a path to follow. The boscage leads into what forms a perfect circle with tree branches reaching and bending in a manner that forms an eye walking straight into the needle. When he breaks the tree line there are red flags periodically set before him in an obscure trail that he follows. Moving funnels the alcohol to all the wrong places inside of him. Sweating and teeth chattering. An image begins to take form when the red flags begin to widen then are all together gone.

Before him stands a large box made of strong wood panels fully closed with nothing to look in or out. Leaves of all color lay around like wildfire. As Trasc circles the cube he counts four shotgun shells in the earth. He draws a cheap snub-nosed .357 revolver and checks the cylinder. Cocks it into single action.

It hangs down at his side. His heart pumping something like lead in his chest. Wishes upon the gun for a striker-fired semiautomatic. Had to sell the rest. Was a believer in the power of the rounds at such distances. The simplicity of design. Was why he kept the shotgun. Cheap, plain, strong. You'd always be outgunned. He saw a silent arms race happening. Everybody wants to be tactical Joe. The guns all anybody has going for them. Pinning himself on the defensive. He didn't like leaving Eudora unarmed. Didn't like the idea of her left alone with it either. Didn't think she'd find any worth in defending herself. He rounds about and sees a side panel of the box dropped away.

Inside there are two dead bodies. They are hand in hand on their backs naked and gone. Trasc never felt a total weakness in the knees such as this.

"If you're going to be late don't come."

There are not many places to hide but he comes out anyway. Trasc backs away from the construct.

"You didn't say anything about this."

"Think about that for a second, kid. Your reaction is to your reaction. Your situation. All things considering. You get what I'm saying here?" Ford says.

"No all I'm..."

"Jesus, kid. Shut the fuck up. You're late. You're dressed like that looking like that. Get out of here. Get a suit and tie."

There was a time of conflict in him. He no longer sought to argue with people. Trasc turns and leaves. His body rebels against him. He finds a clearing and sits against a tree. Feels unreservedly sick. Not booze sick or motion sick. Just simply world sick. Living sick. Work sick. Too much of too little sick. Dumb sick. Shit sick. So fucking sick of being sick.

Everything that can runs from his body. Blisters all around him. There is a hunger and a thirst and a pain and a fear simultaneously happening all at once that seems to create this new and horrible thing.

He focuses on a small spider worlds away on a single blade of grass strung up and acrobatic creating a universe on a string. Looks up at an enormous, abandoned web spun up the tree he leans on. Sleep would have easily taken him if not for this unscalable anguish.

NINE

Lott atop Ro, pounding. When they fuck they remember. What they do is fuck good but other than that they break good. He leaves it in and she holds him there on top of her for a long time. Ro is such a sucker for apologies. The first time he hit her that is exactly what he did. Apologized.

I didn't mean it. I'm sorry. It will never happen again. There is something wrong with me. I'm sorry.

Sorrysorrysorrysorrysorrysorrysorrysorrysorrysorrysorrysorrysorrysorrysorrysorrysorrysorrysorrysorrysorrysorrysorrysorrysorrysorrysorrysorrysorrysorrysorrysorrysorrysorrysorrysorrysorrysorrysorrysorrysorrysorrysorrysorrysorrysorrysorrysorrysorrysorrysorrysorrysorrysorrysorrysorry.

Cycle of pills.

She gave him his back. It all happened again. Again and again and again and again and again and again. She took the apology like a gift. Beg for forgiveness in ways he never did with the boys. He was the bitch who'd get on his knees only for her.

Lott orgasms and dismounts her. Ro breathing heavy as she licks him clean. She wants more. Needs it. She glances at the clock. The apartment reeks of spoil, sex, and sewage. It was hers and he'd just been staying there. Mold as paint. In all the cracks of all the walls, thick black bile forms. Spots of the ceiling and the once carpeted floors of vibrant greens and blues are now yellows and browns. There is no true architectural value to the place at all. Just a box dropped in the middle of the neon New Jersey desert.

She rises from the bed and drapes a robe around her with anime characters on it. She needed to be at the restaurant in an hour. The sex didn't fill the need for something to hold throughout the thirteen hour plus day ahead. Lott pushes her away when she tries to get close. He counts the money from today's job. Besides that he wasn't working. Wasn't throwing anything for rent. Adds it to the cash that Ro claimed to stumble upon. It started the night's affairs. Something like making plans. Ro makes her way to the kitchen.

"Where'd you hit this money. You tell me," Lott says.

"Told you. Stole that shit from down the road. Little gas shop. More for the King, baby. Easy hit. You said you'd get coffee."

"I ain't catching you making them videos again. Slut."

She microwaves breakfast and sets the table. Lott walks in from the hall nervous and bleary eyed. He fixes his boots kicked over by Ro and places them neatly on the mat. Fixes anything that needs straightening. A remote turned slightly on a table. Just walks around in circles. Ro finishes setting the table and moves over to Lott and places a hand on his chest. Lott pushes her away.

Ro watches him assess his surroundings. Studies him, always waiting out his bad vibrations and volatile harmony. He looks at the oatmeal on the tray table accompanied by two steel paint-covered yellow chairs.

"For us?" he says.

"For you. I need to get ready. Can you tidy up the place.

Maybe we can have dinner together when I get home. See about mowing the complex. Help signs all over. They'll take some off rent."

Lott doesn't touch the food. He takes a hit of weed from a bowl on the counter and adjusts blankets and shirts taped to the windows to not let any light in and crawls back in bed.

Ro goes on readying herself for her day. She's talking out loud about the craziness of the restaurant. It was wild to think the supply chain of women there dating not bad but poor men. Weak men. Supporting that cause like charity. She says she wants to see a friend more. Tells him her name is Eudora. Said she looked sad and was new and needed a friend.

Lott gets out of bed hamming up the annoyance of her voice. Throws a laundry basket of folded clothes from the couch and drops into the torn cushions. Flicks on his game console and puts on a headset.

"Move," he says as she tries to kiss him goodbye. "Get the fuck out the way."

And just like that her day begins and ends in idle, rampant movement. Yesterday could have happened today and today could have been just about a hundred years of her future. She hoped it wouldn't last that long. Her jaw ached from grinning. From sucking him. He'd be in her throat all day. Mouth dragged at her feet.

The mosquitoes bite at her ankles walking through the long grass to the door of the apartment when she returns. She'd always ask him to leave the light on. Operating in the dark and fumbling with the keys.

When she steps inside the only thing that changed was the gun and half wasted Evan Williams bottle on the table. Takeout mashed up on the floor that he got with her money. A spent towel adding to the mess at his feet. He'd masturbated. Lott sits in his boxers in the same position playing the same game and cursing into his headset.

"Did you eat?" Ro says.

"I ate."

"Did you get me anything?"

"I don't got money for that shit. Don't you work at a restaurant?"

"I'd pay you back."

"I don't need your money. We should have an open relationship. You pretty much have that already with what you do."

"I don't want to do this tonight."

She heads into the kitchen. Nothing to eat. No water but the brown shit that came from the faucet. Water was his responsibility.

"You're gross," Lott says.

"Me?"

"Fucking pathetic," his eyes on the screen.

Ro heads into the bathroom for a long time. She's tired and hungry and her feet hurt. Smells of sweat and stained all about with food and drink. She falls asleep there on the cold tile floor with the light on.

Lott goes in to take a leak. Leaves her in there. Liked having the bed to himself. She wakes up two hours later. Been having trouble with that lately. Takes a hit and a pull and a pill. Needed to do it all over again in four hours.

TEN

Looking out at the burning country Eudora recalls her father's last words.

Ain't no daughter of mine. Liberal bitch.

He'd speak again in this world. They will not. Everybody looking for reasons to have their petty family shuns. The instrument of her demise lay speculative. His words and their meaning. The gun in his hand pointed her way. His eyes reverberating distant tongue. Irises with a pallet. Sclera polluted. Blues all red washed. To see the world only to swallow all that hate and all that pain to blink it all away.

They're on the road. Trasc behind the wheel. She's in the passenger seat. Red clouds harboring anvils, rust pervades the horizon. Her eyes very much her father's own. They fix on her invisible shadow reflected upon the passenger side window.

Do you see? Do you see your face in the clouds?

Similar storms and tombs within her. Hollow and spectral and weightless. Tempest heart. She feels haunted. Something holding feast within her snatching away the simplest of desires and joys. Across the obscurity this way of the eastern sky the false horizon is lit with flashes of gunfire. She imagines the sky falling and blanketing it all away.

"You want to talk about it?" he says.

"About what?"

"About anything."

"We've been driving a long time. I'm just tired."

"You're always tired. Slept the whole way. Slept half your life away last two years, Eu."

"That's not the problem."

"What is?"

"I keep waking up."

"Come on."

"I'm fine."

"Got a smile like a broken record. Like something in the wiring is wrong. Your mouth moves but it don't reach your eyes. Like something disconnected."

"Look away. Desperate clinging upon such desperate terrain tell you right quick. You watch a world lose their mind and you go on and you follow. Nihilism is contagious. The truth of all things revealed at last."

"How the white knight has fallen. Dragged down to our level. Dug a grave at rock bottom."

"What does that mean?"

"You used to not think that way. I just want to know if you're okay."

"Stop asking me that."

"Your father pointed a gun at you."

"He didn't know it was loaded. And he was drunk."

"Point blank."

"Remember the time you got yourself the shotgun."

"I'm not sure I can fully grasp what from fuck all."

"Almost blew your hand off."

"The fact that it happened. Or the fact that you didn't flinch. We just ignore the whole thing. Pretend it didn't happen. You... you thanked him. You thanked him for it. Are we going to sit here like that's normal? Did you know he wouldn't shoot?"

"He did shoot."

"Right."

Silence abided by the sounds of the road. Roiling by one another in perfidious toiling. Drifting through a monotonous canal that rises from these coastal depths. None the way of mountains or plains. Tumors metastasizing across the canvas of these common grounds of desolation. All the tracks left behind these travelers carrying ex-lives sewn within those treads left on the concrete of severed dreams and astray naivety. NJ-33 to the Garden State Parkway. County Highway 508 onwards to NJ-10. Every mile-marker reminded her just how menial it all had come to be. How everything looked the same.

It stays that way for quite some time on the cold and nothing same road. Very quiet despite all the forward movement. The car began to swallow any hindsight. Like being at the bottom of a pool. Not looking up but looking ahead. Looking at that blurry aquatic grayness in spite of the sun. Taking it to the face.

The darkness takes to the sky. Trasc follows Eudora's gaze ignited by electric purple with ink black clouds huge and holographic crawling over the parkway. The truck sits high and above vehicles. It proposes some form of likeness not having to look at another human face.

"I used to know this girl," Eudora says, "had a pet snake. Thing stopped eating. Four trips to the vet with no clarity. Snake keeps starving itself. She'd wake to it out of its cage. A few more trips. Nothing. Nights come to pass the thing is in bed with her. Beside her. Straight down her leg. Repeat. Doc trip. Tells her there's nothing wrong. Not starving itself. Not sick. It's getting ready to eat her. This country. Every love every friendship. Every petulant hate and unfulfillment. Every politician and fortuneteller and salesman. Family. All I see are people trying to eat each other."

He's still. Says nothing. Eyes forward.

"I need to go to the bathroom," she says.

"This is rough country."

"It all is. Can't hide from it. Just stop."

"Fake it till you make it, right?"

"Right."

"We came up here for your family, Eu. To be closer to them. I told you this would happen."

"We came up here because we had nowhere else to go. Nothing else to do."

"When I was young I was too aware of our hypocrisies. Nobody knows nobody. Nobody cared if I was around. Then I didn't care. There's a shadow on your family. This dark thing. Like silent loaded guns hanging over your heads. It was only a matter of time. I told you they didn't give a shit about us."

"Stop."

"About you."

"I said stop it. You don't get to say that."

"Come up this way. All of us so close together and still so far apart. They have the hospitality of a funeral director. Like dining with a dead animal in the road. Gutter class."

"You always know everything."

"Don't I."

"Jesus."

"Hey. Look. I love you."

"I know."

"It's a fresh start. We can start over. Always talked about coming out this way. We have a lot to be excited about. I'm excited. It'll be okay. Everything is okay."

The way self-realizations of terrify land at your feet. Eudora realized that optimism seemed a great weight too heavy to hold. Too big a lie to tell. When certain truths or neurotic depression found their way to line the walls of your arteries there'd be no way of cheapening them.

"Slow down," Eudora says.

"Ain't no police. Nobody's pulling us over."

"Stop the car."

He looks around for an overpass. They pass a dead body. Things like this normalizing the slow decay and logical flow of bodies disassociated from the souls trapped inside them. Dogs of war and all their running gone to seed. Meshuga inhabitance of a world gone by. Impossible not to feel the coming decline. He's looking at his phone before the world smoke rises from the settling tires. Dying wild fireweed through cracks in the earth. Sacrificial habituations of one's very own head.

There's no service. No power of charge but that from the sun. That lonely and distant and cowering star defiant in its own insular hanging. Rebel to every hour cowering in the sky. The artificiality brings solace from about the hallucinatory futility of it all. Drag and drop the screen, zoom in, and reveal the depravity of the world coming to be come to pass. Autonomized pixilation and avatars under meek lambency. The devolving of a species to a land of aesthetic degeneracy. The flatness of it all. Austere only to grave decadence. If not to look away. If not much worth the attention of these expiring eyes. To be the only one to watch the sun burn out and the moon to fall and to feel all that tired twirling and every single thing and every thought turned black but one white exit sign. Float away in serenity.

"Hurry up. Be careful. We're almost home," Trasc says and hands her the revolver.

ELEVEN

The gravel in her gut stirs. Silence cast out the barren woodlands like something tangible. Light weaving its way through nature's architectural terrain dispensed by some great arm of some otherworldly being slicing and severing the shadows and the dark with great sheens of light. All this abstract illumination. The sky not one color but many. There is no birdsong. The forest wind casts itself outward as if to avoid human contact. A wet and very light snow sifts way to some other landings. Takes away anything somber about it.

Only the mechanical birds of man cascading past to dispense unto the distant below. The sounds of skin tearing from bone ripping the skies from out of place and dropping their contributions for the dying and the dead. That eternal rest formed of new element taking its shape. Air weaving through the trees like a current. Nothing else grows if not for them rising like stripped and cold and shapeless bars of this natural penitentiary. Such innate features one might find it the void. She'd consider if one might go blind having never seen any beauty in the world.

Acrid sensations on her exposed flesh. The passing gale

more a substance. Oily and strange. The temperature seems to change with each gust. Elements in contortion with reverberations of a constant and distant thrumming of hurricanes. She's dressed too thinly. Her clothes ragged and worn. She considers the where and the when. In truth, she cannot recall the last day or the last time she's recalled much of anything. Can't place where and when that happened.

She believed that you begin to lose control by measures governed in varying degrees of certain reconciliatory natures. She liked the sound of the distant train that wakes her in the new house. Trasc has yet to spend the night. She liked to think of it as something calling to her. Piping away at the bygone commuter station she can hear but could not see. She tried but often found that it was difficult to ponder the concepts of your own life. Hers lay in the valley of death and love. Eudora was divided upon that lonely lane of crumbling mountains where no light rests any which way of that isolated tunnel. She'd not considered in her young mortality and astray naivety along the cruel streets she walks unaccompanied just how much these themes would subsume the final stretch.

When you are to reconcile yourself to dying and integrating yourself with the shroud all declaratory imitations of claim to this world render themselves conceptual. What becomes of the now is that of a warped memory. Reverence for what is never to be falling in line with what has never been done or will do again.

Nothing short of the feeling of having swallowed a bucket of nails. She regards the book in her hand. Tears out a page. Reaches behind her. Looking down at the desecrated soil she sees reds and blacks having left her body where they should not lay. Her abdomen grinds. She takes out a small plastic jar of pills. She's running low. Makes her nervous. She didn't want to die just yet. But she didn't want to be sober either.

This seemed no time to quit. She considers filling the palm of her hand. Takes two instead.

Looking at the tree line where she entered this sad forest she can no longer see Trasc or the truck or the clearing. A disturbance in the rhythms of the foliage, dirt, ash. A strange and twisted tree over the bluff where she entered and fixed her gaze as to not get lost in turn gets lost in shadow as darkness begins to stretch. She takes out a lighter. Sets the book on fire. Tosses it into the root rot corroding the forest floor watching the annosus and armillaria root spin purple gold and dance atop this ashy graveyard. Small twigs break beneath her every step like tiny pieces of broken wooden glass. To fall deep from where she stood through the cracks of the earth. What would burgeon and grow from such a grave. What would become of the roots she feeds.

She regards the burning book as a meaningless and useless object. In memory the very thing set by other tools and other hands within her own heart of what forever in reality had been only a pretense of an attribute. Of what use of it was ever anything to anybody. They're just words. To her it all cleared way to only suicidal definitions. Facilitated manufactured purposes and meanings.

Pyramids. Language and the book. The atom bomb. Proceeding one another yet the finite rests only in conception of devastating ends. Her own thoughts always galloping too far ahead of her. Trasc had mentioned something set two years from now and it made Eudora sweat and feel something just shy of dizzy. She wanted to laugh at the idea that anything could be happening ahead of the time she currently loathed. There was a world of blackness and nothingness far gone into her needs. Anything else seemed an unreality.

The decline has been that of the human mind where no book could reach at all. Without the invention of the mere catalyst of its being the book could not be and that vital cog of all our telling and all our ideology shackled to the counter that is its benediction and its contrast. One last thing for that road. She despised everything. Tried to focus on her breathing and clear her head but it just made her want to scream and get it all out.

Rolling, clapping gunfire rattles the way she came. Thunderous and closer and coming from above and all sides. A sky so black it's almost blue lighting the earth in banishment of a sun that has not yet set. A motorcade. Vehicles beyond the trees. Engine and chatter in greater number alike. She hears Trasc calling out to her.

Human heat and urgency rustling through the dead earth. An enormous man appears before her. His skin is dark and painted in red brushed all about him. His eyes blacked out in coal. A rust-colored bright orange streaks his thick black hair. In peripheral glancing she'd might mistake him for a great Douglas-fir or a bear. What lay deceased crosses over maimed. He carries a man over his thick neck and shoulders.

Eudora takes a step back. Keeps her weight on her toes. She should have eaten something. Lightheaded and weak. The man is breathing hard. He supports the man over his shoulder and in his other hand holds a weapon made from wood and steel about half her length. More weapons line his belt and thighs that are the size themselves of trunks. The country seems to shrink in his presence. Trasc calls her name again. Another explosion.

She doesn't move. The chatter rises from the road. Imbecile language. He drops the game from around his shoulders. He'd been tense but something in him loosens. Reaches into his belt and pulls out a shaved and jagged piece of timber. Movement rattles the trees above. Cold sweat runs down her spine. Her own lungs hijacked.

The forest makes the sounds of unhinged laughter. Something small and living scurries across the ground. He does not take his eyes off her as he throws the piece of timber at the ground. She takes a step back from his point of action. Looks up then back at him then to the road and back at him again. He doesn't move. Says something to her in a language she does not know.

Eudora follows his dark eyes to the dead American pika at her feet. Floods out west brought about unnatural migrations only to find the same seasickness coast to coast. The man repeats his words. Squares himself with her. Steps forward and repeats himself again. In her terror she'd forgotten she's armed. She pulls out the .357. The hammer gets tagged by her shirt. It's heavy in her hand. Shows him that it's there but keeps it low at her side.

He keeps on coming. She can feel the heat radiating off his body when he's close. Her hands are cold, robbing them of their instrumental value. He's placed his palm over his belly at rest. Thunder coils overhead and the light, gelatinous, almost pinkish snow continues falling but never seems to touch the ground. The earth grown weary. Nothing thunderous about this cold echoing rataplan. Indigestion in the haggard sky. The man says something once more in relic tongue.

"Get off of me."

He repeats his words.

"Get your hands off of me."

Repeating.

She backs away. The man takes out a joint and lights it and hits it and passes it her way. Eudora takes it and smells it. Hits it twice. He repeats his ancient words as they affirm from reasoning to sermon. A whisper and a prayer. By and by the whole thing turns spectacle. Something of a song. He waves his hands over her. Strikes something alight then holds a candle flame he'd pulled from about his person over her as if to guide her from about some dark.

He seems to be wafting and fanning and setting free some great ghost from out of her. He dances. Moves around her, pounding his chest. He is chanting. Picking up her waste and the earth that cradles it and throwing it away with a howl. Reaches into a slit of his tethered skirt around his jeans and claps a plume of yellow dust around her. Nothing sacred and no sorcery of divinity would reach to such depths of her own despair. Such the source of her pain needing excavation from the boneyard wasteland that lay underneath her flesh.

"Stop," she says.

He continues on.

"I said stop."

Dancing. He is dancing.

"STOP."

She turns to face him. He's ceased his ritual, frozen in midstride of the last bodily strokes of his movements with the joint in his mouth. His lips are pursed, eyes gone astray. She tries to fight it but it bursts out of her. She begins to laugh. Full bellied. He straightens out and the two laugh together. Concussive blasts the way she came. She tucks away the revolver.

"I forgot the sound of that."

The man reaches down and picks up the photo album left in the dirt by the burned book. He begins to leer over the photos. Looks away and reaches the photo album toward her and she takes it. He says something. She shakes her head. He pats his heart. Points to the album and cradles his chest and smiles.

"Should come with a disclaimer. Careful. Frangible," she more so speaks to herself as she packs her things.

He shakes his head. Reaches down into thick wool socks pulled high over his painted legs. Mere draping of torn and ragged cloth. It all looks to be homemade. He pulls out a photograph of a woman and shows it to her.

"That what you're out for?"

"Home."

"That where she is?"

He smiles and taps the face of the woman inside the picture. "Home."

Flyovers tearing through the skies. Another blast. A veil seems to wash over the mirrored ecstasy. It all resembles some depressionist piece to her. An upside-down oil spill, this drunken masterpiece and sparkling demise. The sky seems poisoned by some celestial cavity.

She considers that we are the sum of the stories that we can tell. Fictitious hollow actualities of the time there is none to spare. She circles around as if there's much to gather.

"You know the story of Zeus visiting the elderly couple?"

They lock eyes.

"Married all those years. The wife gone only a few days before the husband. Zeus came as a traveler. The two over supper sharing with him their greatest fear. Being without the other. This life or the next. In their passing their home grew intertwining trees growing up the sides. Like locked hands," Eudora takes in the nature around them. Eyes scaling the trees. "Can you tell me which were friends and which were lovers? Just how long they've been keeping each other company. Of what I will become? Of this earth or of another blackness. Will the tree have eyes? Give it a name," she bites her lower lip and begins to cry. "I was going to leave. But I never did."

The man reaches towards her. She doesn't fight it. He catches a tear on his thumb and runs it across her face in the shape of an X. Whispers something to himself. He pats his chest.

"Ahiga-Tsela-Tahoma."

Eudora doesn't move. Doesn't say anything.

"Ahiga," drumming of his heart.

"Ahiga," Eudora says.

"Tsela-Tahoma."

She repeats after him and he smiles at that.

"Eudora," she pats her own chest.

The man shakes his head. Extends two fingers her way upon the outstretched hand. She sees now as their eyes meet that he cries for her. He gives her a name. Speaks slowly and methodically.

"Celvi-Qui-Pant-Dans-Des-Chemins-Longs-Et-Sombre-Et-Don't-On-Espere-Qu'll-Ponre-Revenir."

"Okay."

He looks at her smiling.

"You want me to write that down?"

He does.

"I wasn't serious."

Holds it her way.

"Thanks."

A wheezing coming back to consciousness.

"My fucking head. Christ. You cherry prick," the voice is slurred and delirious.

Face down and crawling in a pool of blood his own or the likes of someone or something else. On his back is a large skull insignia. Pure Americana, a group she recognizes. Bands and hordes of too many militias and tribes roaming the streets as migrants of no nation, no creed. Only that of the mindless. The heartless. The corrupted and bankrupted of virtues. The man moves past her and places his boot on the other man's back.

"Fuck off me gut-eater."

The man reaches for cable around his torso. Ties the man's hands behind his back. Picks him up and over his shoulder and is gone.

She figures she just might have imagined the whole thing. Everything sags around her and the silence returns. Any beckoning of her name goes distorted outside the metrics of the physicality of her own occupancy. Every bit of nature hangs weak spined and weeping. She stands in the middle of it all.

Picking up her things from the dirt Eudora sees he's left a hunk of rabbit's belly by the photo album. She picks up the photo album and opens it. Textured writing engraving the inside cover. Eudora's words.

Not our first book and not our last. Every love story is a ghost story. We will haunt each other. Love is one long conversation until you run out of things to say. You fall in love with another's silence. These pictures tell our story in the silence they keep. Fiercely and passionately. Our shadows will run forever. Hand in hand.

She flips through it. The pictures seem to move and dance as she does. Then they become very still. She's noticed their appearances changing. Something happening to beauty. Not a stomping out but a dimming of the color and light. Heavy anvil eyes. Paled skin. Smiles receding and alcohol in every picture and weight gained. She'd thought she aged a thousand years in the last two. Remembered a time where petty things like feeling pretty mattered. She walked with a confidence until one day she didn't and realized that altogether our fears and worries and stresses stole things from us little by little.

There is a last photograph of only her looking like something she could not put a label to but something that only made her angry and sad. She considers how many emotional untruths and lies one might die with buried beneath them. The dark was absolute and at the middle of it all was Trasc. A blackbird hovers high overhead and circling her. She tastes blood on her teeth.

TWELVE

Out of the woods and into the clearing. Three soldiers, all men. The van parked right where they left it. A pull off hole in the world of intertwining roads all over these twisting valleys. Shaped like a dead-end cul-de-sac down a scale of fat Engelmann spruces and taller green mountains with a sky gold burned magenta with flecks of oversized ash harboring a few electric clouds. The only natural beauty of the world with semblance to truth is that very road leading nowhere but back the way they came. Sagebrush and buffaloberry shrubs line the encampment. All life down to the plants themselves seem to be gasping for air. That rancid snow kicks up again. It feels like a needle headache all throughout the body.

"There she is," one of the soldiers says. "We was waiting on you."

Sweat in the cold running down her back. Her body nothing but glass. Her eyes ball like fists within those sockets looking for Trasc.

The small market is pitch dark. A run down, broken, ransacked little place. Nothing comes from inside. Nothing moves. All terrain has gone and matched its counterparts that walk amongst them. Abandoned as if everything in audience stands as monuments on reverting land. No door and no sign. Broken glass and remnants from looters remain. It was slim pickings for everybody. Beggars never able to be choosers.

Eudora sometimes slipped out the back of her head and considered how many colors framed her being. Here it is but two. A silver green and date brown. Vague and lifeless smells. She steps toward the vehicle. Coming out from the vegetation and Edenic nature of all that burnt foliage prior she can't help but drown in this new wide open. The van seems miles away. Presents itself as a mirage. She hammers on.

"That's it. Come on. Know what I'm saying? We're starving. Know what I'm saying?" a soldier says.

"Even if we got to settle for a spoiled little thing," the second.

"Shit. You look haunted, honey," the third.

The third of the lot steps from around the vehicle. She's close enough to see their faces. All of them wield rifles. None of the uniforms fit right. Two of them are tattooed on their faces and necks with shaved heads. One steps forward. He's laughing a terrible snicker through a heinous sneer with matted green hair that does not move and is filthy and uncombed. Just keeps chuckling to himself and hitting a vape with a rifle hung at single point.

He throws something into the air. The other soldiers hit the ground. Then it's all drained away. Everything submerged in falling sun. Heat everywhere. Never such a light.

There is everything then there is nothing then there is everything again. All senses tear away from her genetic coding. Each sensation burned to her. The sanctity of life recalibrated and brought back.

The explosion rocks her but the toss was high enough to form a clearing. A small pinwheel of fire opening up within feet of them. Right above them. Feeling the heat like an invitation. It's something homemade with no shrapnel.

Eudora ponders the immediacy or certain pain and the diversity in the latter. It's that bottom feeder type of pain that rests beneath the surface. A creature of no mind and with no eyes waiting in the dark. She wouldn't deal with it. If it were to depart her metrics she'd seek it out. There was too long an uncertainty but always a knowing.

"You see? I'm talking, like, yea, you see? Shit, bro. I mean, right? That one went high," the thrower says. He reaches into his pocket and grabs something inside and sticks it in his mouth and sucks on it. "I blew up God."

"I told you. Chill with that shit," Honey Boy says.

Trasc and two other men in police uniforms move on down the road toward them.

"That's no police," Eudora says.

"No?" one of the policemen says.

"No."

"Well. We it now," a soldier says.

"That what you're doing out here?" Trasc says.

"We patrol when we can."

Trasc puts a hand on Eudora's shoulder in greeting. Comforts her with a smile. "We were clearing out the shop."

"That what you do when you have time off? Blow shit up," Eudora says.

"I think it's what we do when we are working, too."

"What's it been? A year since the strike?"

"Who's counting?"

"Revealed at last what's always been. A thuggish and ignorant militia free roaming the diverse deserts in the heartsick idiot war."

"Eu," Trasc says.

She considers labeling them by identifying tattoos. One of the cops, Cross. The other, Spider. We have Honey Boy, our introductory man. The Jester, our pyrotechnic engineer. And then the last soldier. Only a boy so skinny he seems to be just a floating confused head swallowed by his drags. He hasn't said anything. Cannot maintain eye contact for long periods of time.

She didn't hear him come upon the scene. The man prior stands at the tree line, warden to these trespassers. Without his prisoner. The wind shifts. It ignites her senses like napalm.

The man takes out a six inch .10mm Dan Wesson. Small etchings down the slide. To her messy vision he seems to be holding a sort of instrument. He begins to play it. At first like an untuned violin string in the dark. Then an eruption of sound.

Father's last words. *These things don't matter anymore*, he'd say in drunken slurs. *It's all going away. All of it shot to shit.*

"Big dog," Honey Boy says. He lets out the howl of a wolf. "Where's our man? We need our guy, hoss."

Just like that. How quick. To be here and then not to be here. Shakespeare wept at our conundrum. This great charade of human predicament. Where do you go when the lights go out? When the night caves in.

The men raise their hands and back away with a certain reluctant apathy. With the housing crisis and rise of tent cities came certain retributions. Atoning land seizures. This became Northern Arapaho territory. Eudora and Trasc move closer together. Back away toward the truck.

The man shouts uninterpreted convictions.

"What'd you do to him?" Eudora says.

"Least he's authentic," Honey Boy says. He gathers his things. The men begin to move on. "Entering some tribalistic times, hon. All the minimal. The violent and the disconnected. The detached and the deranged. He all mad about a pipeline. Golly, I tell you, man, I tell you. If social justice ain't no type of justice at all but a hijacking. Bored crusaders."

Trasc brushes Eudora's shoulder and climbs into the van. Eudora stares into the sun that seems unable to push away her eyes and she cannot remember the warm embrace and recalls only the fire. She rounds the van and knocks on the trunk and it pops open. She takes out the shotgun, shuts the door, and gets into the passenger seat with the shotgun across her lap.

"You okay?" Trasc asks.

"I'm fine. You?"

"I'm fine."

THIRTEEN

Somewhere along the way they circled back around. They'd be further from the beaches. Wanted to see them off.

"Don't know what you got until it's gone, you know?" Trasc says.

"You hate the beach."

"But you like it."

"Oh yeah. Bodies of water. Wow. I'll make a wish. I'll wish for a point."

"Why is there no point?"

"You probably can't even drive up."

"You can drive up."

"How far?"

"Until we meet the water."

"That water come meet you."

"I don't think like that."

"Like what?"

"Like you do. Negatively. Like you do."

"Why do you always get so worked up when we talk. Why can't we just talk? It's not good for you."

Fat highway with empty lanes filling the dash. Sky spilling before them like a black tongue swallowing yellow stars. Long silence along that hard road. They'd traveled north and at one point the drive felt like a literal climb. Actual muscle fibers recruited to take certain turbulences. Getting boots on the ground they found that the elevation heightened if anything a sense of a rotational pull. If anything at all Eudora got used to it. A cave cricket chases a shadow across the dash.

"Eudora, wait."

She picks up a thick hardcover of Sylvia Plath's collected letters and gets rid of the bug.

"Why'd you do that?"

"Oh yeah," more breath than word from Eudora, "no killing. You found God. Whoever She is."

"It ain't spun like that."

"It's spinning? Which way is it spinning?" Eudora is aghast. Hams it up and mimes genuine shock. "It's a bug."

"Certain cultures say killing them brings bad luck."

"My culture it's good."

"It's moving it's living."

"That so?"

"What happened to you?"

"You. You happened to me."

Autopilot as she moves out into the road. She'd been waiting for sleep world to befall her. Would ping pong from one useless conversation and menial task totally aware of their uselessness and seemed absolutely unbelieving in the whole process. It was an impossible endurance to keep living like that.

Rocks and water, an ocean at large. A bluff of sorts. Then wet and cold grass. It was covered three feet in water that was up pretty much to the main road line. Waves too close for comfort. The sky wraps around everything with a total black around that like some other thing attached to it. She felt irritated that her shoes had become wet.

She was spoken to throughout the journey. Trasc's voice a directionless whisper. What was there to say to one another after all this time? There's a mist around everything, cold and salted, a greenish and rusty hue. More so than sand she feels wet soil and grass. The road stretches beneath. The sound of waves immense and total.

She props herself up on her elbows on the truck. On a bluff and down through lower dunes to a wheat grove. The city itself has become a sunken pit with a wide variation of entry points. Something you just sort of came up on driving along the coast.

No beginning and no road leading or ending save anyplace but this vision of the entirety of a collapsing Atlantic City. It all looked like a single apocalyptic beach. Something consumed and adrift as if being taken up by some supernatural disaster. The buildings stand flaccid and carried off into the distant nowhere like dandelion sparks. Broad construction obscured in the haze of things gone wrong left alone in this foggy myriad of some strange dream and forgotten town. Moving slowly through the flood. You would think nobody had ever been here at all or ever shared any memories as the way a city dies and the world keeps spinning. All these hedged bets paid off.

Around them lay white lilies frail and small. Frozen and preserved in the earth like some needed memory. Around the beach things lay rotten. They sit atop the hood of the truck.

This sort of fatigue or manic episodes would fall on her. Her voice projects from not much more than a shadow or a shape. A lethargic and disinterested and unfulfilled amoeba where all light receded and never moved toward. Like what was inside a strange and black shell canvased in the cold wet sand before them.

She sees the floating carnival not too far off down the valley and out into the sea about fifty yards. Arriving through a canal to and from some desecrated and nameless ocean bringing you from one corroded coast to the next. Bringing one to the other. All lights and golden glitz. She cannot help ponder the sea and the stars and in such navigation to which gelid darkness she'd like to rather resign.

"I almost got us tickets to one of those."

"What?"

Eudora points at the cruise. "Something like *The Cruise at the End of the World*."

"It ain't the end of the world."

"What are they saying. Something like ten years? The supervolcano or whatever they found."

"It's not like that. We'll begin again."

Everything collides. Down the beach a house on stilts collapses into the ocean. It looks to be worth something and habitable. They watch the two-story house take sail trekking the hungry sea.

"I hope no one is in there," Trasc says.

"Why?"

"Why what?"

"I think just sort of drifting out there with nobody around doesn't seem like such a bad thing. The purple of your heart floods with dissatisfaction crack a window. Sink right into the ocean."

"Christ."

"Where?"

"Jesus."

"Wept."

"Alright."

A beat between them as they get lost in the waves.

"We are lucky. This house we're moving in just fell into our lap," Trasc says.

"You're very lucky."

"I still got shit I got to deal with. Shit I got to take."

"Least you give a shit about something."

"Eudora."

She turns away. The salt and condensation in the air masks her tears. "Everything is just so shitty. Everybody is so miserable all the time."

"It doesn't need to be that way."

"It is not a way of being. It's just what is."

"Being alone is like being with a mistress. You let it in and it'll have you question the worth of people. Give it enough time even the ones you thought you needed. Need to be careful with that. Coming back is hard."

"A good mistress keeps unsolved mends in a relationship."

Thick clouds move about cascading a landing to swallow all in their wake. Ambient, no wind chill, very dry despite the ocean. Eudora considers them. Trasc tries to connect with her eyes.

"They each carry a hurricane. A levee left unattended to wash it all away. You wonder just how much our hearts can hold. How much they can take. All of it gone asunder," Eudora says.

"We'll ride it out. I'm done fucking around. I came back to you and left it all behind because I'm done. And we're only just beginning. We can start over. I've been a fool."

"You're laced with regrets."

"What's that supposed to mean?"

"Nothing."

"You left."

"I didn't leave you."

"Okay."

"Your tendencies have become my sin. I wish I never met you."

"Don't say that. I can't live without you."

"Don't say that."

"Why not?"

"Just don't say it."

"It's true."

"No hope survives here. Hope has become bitter on my tongue."

"There's got to be a way to see this through with you."

"You used to be my fallen angel."

"That's the problem. I knew coming out here you would see my deficiencies."

"Now you're just all clipped wings. All fall down. The other day at the restaurant I had a guy. White wine and muscles for himself. Buried his wife that day. Said watching her on her death bed he knew he was bound to wreckage with her passage. He started to cry as I was taking his order and I apologized out of habit and to tell you the truth I was a little annoyed by him and that annoyed me about myself."

"Shit like that. You used to have more patience with people."

"His wife had thyroid surgery before she died. Had her throat cut. This swinging scalpel hanging over our throats. This process of incisions. It's unavoidable. Can't keep up with the cutting. This train we're on. I would've opted out of the surgery. Better yet. Stop at the slit. Let me bleed out."

"You're too hard on yourself. On everything. Just too hard. It must be terrible inside your head."

"Chalk it up for another robbery. Mourners are the hardened. We were never meant for long relationships. Not meant to grieve like this. I'm tired of feeling this way."

"Why does it have to always come back to that? You make joy impossible. You make staying impossible. You make leaving impossible you make loving impossible you... you are impossible, Eudora."

"So, his great love is on that bed made to carry you off into the dark and he's crying and telling me that he doesn't want to leave yet. His wife couldn't turn her head. He wanted another shot at the whole thing, being a bit at the end of the rope. Doesn't want to know what death is. Like he was making it about him. He called it a ride. That life was like a ride and he wanted to go again. Again and again and again. I'd hoped he was wrong. That these aren't merry-go-round lives. Some kind of loop."

"It's not that bad."

"You're right. It's worse."

"Jesus."

"You always needed chaos."

"No. I just need you."

"Maybe they're one and the same."

"Jesus."

"You keep saying his name. Do you think he'll answer?"

"Alright."

Trasc gets up as the water rises around them in steady approach. Thick clouds of toxic fumes roll atop the filthy water like tumbleweeds of smoke. Complications all over the state with the drinking water. Signs across the country. NO MONEY. NO MORE FOOD. NO MORE MEDICINE. DO NOT DRINK.

The water is up to the tires. A light, rhythmic tapping on the side. Eudora and Trasc round the bend of the grill. A body face down in the water. Skin telling them he's been in there a long time. Traveled a long way.

"How's this happen?" Eudora says.

"I don't know."

"Let's go."

"We should bury him."

"He's already buried. It's all buried."

Trasc sets to loading the vehicle and checking the oil and

the tires. He hasn't told her much because he knew it'd fall on deaf ears and he'd been trying to give up the preacher front and save every last breath. It seemed a time to preserve such. Speak when spoken to. Only nobody seemed to ever have anything to say. Even life and death circumstances brings about a collective cumulative shrug. He's telling her about his work with Ford and the Boxman and a dream he's been having.

"He puts them inside I think to see... gosh, I don't know what. We tracked some adolescent killings that might be linked to him. Maybe a him. An origin. Started in people's homes. A sort or social experiment to see what guys would lay down their lives for their families. Their wives. Which ones were cowards. Been having this dream. Me and you inside one of them things. Not together. In our own. It's terrible and we are so alone and so cold and it gets difficult to breathe with nowhere to come up for air and the walls begin to speak and shake. I find and clutch stray grass yarn just rubbing it between my fingertips. You find a nail or a splinter and you... you..."

When Trasc rises up crouched aside the last tire he finds himself no company. He turns about and calls to Eudora and sees she'd set off down to the water stripped and walking in. He can feel the cold about it just as witness. Her name frozen in his throat. Futility in any rebuttal. He doesn't call out to her. Just watches her walking on in and under, barely keeping her head above water. The sea reflects a moon so total and the stars lens themselves all across the surface of the water that it seems as though she's set a path to some other universe having torn apart her own, taking his and everything with it.

FOURTEEN

The humming of window heating units filled the silence between them. Maybe those using woodchips or oil. It would be Trasc's first night at the house with Eudora. The drive out to the restaurant where Eudora works is only a hair plus of ten minutes. He pulls over for gas. Knows that it drops him below two hundred dollars to his name. He'd probably hit his peak. He had a book and it was small and just everything about the whole business had him feeling a bit grifter society. But it added to his mystic when it needed to. Small talk on that.

The restaurant is closed but Daniella invited them. She valued Eudora's commitment and hard work. Eleven doubles in a row. Eudora and Ro were in correspondence. Lott and John made it out. All six voyagers into the dark.

The night brought about disappointing tidings. Genocide of aluminum and glass. They were all pretty much in the bag. Everybody but Trasc. He saved his. Never understood social drinking. He liked to sit in the murk by himself.

The restaurant impressed him. It was historic grounds, a mansion. Daniella used to live in it but moved on from that lifestyle. Inside seating makes it feel so that it is homey and cozy with a bar that has that dive bar, one last bender, one final night darkly lit vibrance to it. Outside is where things really come alive. Farmland and lights hung every which way. Firepits and bars designed to fit the bill. They stand on their feet around open flame. When all spoils run dry the wine keeps on pouring.

"Come on, come on. Thank you for coming. Thank you, thank you," John pours all around.

"And for all the hard work," Daniella says twirling her hand in the wind to the soft music.

"Tyrant," John says.

They all laugh. Trasc can't help but notice in those small moments who is authentic with their laughter and just how quickly it recedes away. He watches it on Eudora all the time. Like she premeditated every smile just to get by.

"It's really been divine," Ro says.

"Divine," Eudora says.

"That's a lot, right?"

"Maybe."

"Still. The gusto. Coming out like that."

"How do you mean?"

"I don't know. You look like you're kind of on the couch and not on a date. Like you don't like the person you're with."

"Ouch. Spicy," Daniella says.

"It's okay. It's why we get along," Ro says.

"I didn't put two and two together," John says.

"What's that?" Trasc says.

"Small world. Talking to him. Getting to know you. You met with a buddy of mine."

"Ford?"

"Yeah."

"Swell guy."

"Swell."

"He's probably a bit pissed at me."

"That's probably how I feel all the time. He was supposed to be here tonight. You're a bit all over the place. Career wise."

"It's a good opportunity. None of them feel like careers."

"Can you read me? Tell me what I do."

"What you did or what you do?"

"I don't copy."

"You're asking me what you did."

"That then. Sure."

"I don't think it works that way."

"Which way does it?"

"John," Daniella says.

"You never thought to ask your pal, Ford?"

Eudora scoffs.

"What?" Trasc says.

"Pals. Friends. What is such a thing. Better off finding a unicorn."

"She's funny like that," Daniella says.

Neon laughs. Ro scrolls through her phone. Daniella is up and taking dishes. Eudora is doing that thing where she plays the listener. She just floats along in this bubble. He would think that if anybody ever looked closely they'd be able to see it. Maybe they just never voiced it. Her family surely seemed oblivious. Every word she ever spoke always seemed to take on an insurmountable effort. Sometimes looking as though she were straining to keep her eyes open. Lott and Ro that couple that believe nobody can see or hear them bickering. Erupting in small bouts and tantrums from time to time at the table and now here over the fire. Daniella comes back with a tray of shot glasses.

"Pudding wine. We have wine bottles for you on your way home."

Everybody takes their small glass and kicks back.

"What are you going to school for?" John asks Ro.

"Social justice," she's tipsy and it shows in her voice.

She keeps playing with Lott's hair a way he doesn't like. Keeps swatting away at her hand in ways that makes everybody uncomfortable. John swallows the rest of his glass and pours more. Offers the bottle to everybody else but they decline. Opens his eyes wide and shakes his head beckoning Ro along.

"I just think that like if you start looking into this country and things it's crazy how we can be a country with the stuff that we did. Like mass incarceration. The industrial military complex."

"Military-industrial complex," Daniella says.

"Exactly."

"I don't know. My father was Spanish-Italian. Came to this country, his father before him. Didn't speak English besides some racial slurs until he was eight years old. My wife comes from Portugal. Successful woman. You work at her restaurant," John says.

"Pretty insensitive, man," Lott says.

"There he is. Not much the talker."

"I like learning."

"I bet. I bet you're real good at learning things. I get nervous about you guys, you know. The youths. As they say."

"Think we're doing okay."

"I know. I'm just teasing. What's your book about, Adonis."

"You can call me Trasc."

"Got it."

"You're not supposed to ask that, John," Daniella says.

"How's the new house? You liking the area?"

"Sure."

"Sleeping? Hearing all the new sounds and everything."

"Try to. Gotta be on your toes these days."

"That you do. Salvador Dali believed that all you needed

to survive was to lose consciousness and instantly regain it. Would sleep deprive himself by sleeping in a wooden chair with a brass key in his hand. When he dropped the key, he woke up," John says.

"Tells this story all the time," Daniella says.

"Look at them all. They're captivated."

Trasc smiles and it falls away when people stop looking.

"I have just become so unamazed by you," Daniella says to John smearing cream over his face.

"So say we all. Hear, hear," John takes a folded piece of cloth collecting dust off a table and swats away at the surface. Stands on the table and takes a knee. "Finally, we come forth. Dare I say, dare I say it, ladies and gentlemen. Love lies in the throes of rhetoric."

"This place needs to be shut down. I need to go back to my country," Daniella says.

Everyone is animated about the whole thing. Radical ideas on the foundations of love and the relationships that we undermine. John going on about how it's a heroic sacrifice for a man to devout themselves to a single lover. How a man is wedlock to barbaric intents right from the cord.

Trasc tries to find Eudora's eyes to see if they can split. Hasn't made much eye contact with him the whole night. She'd beg him to come to things like this and ignore him when they'd be there after getting angry that he didn't want to come.

"I used to like my husband, I did," Daniella says.

"We liked each other," Ro says. Throws an arm around Lott. "Living with one another is hard."

"It shouldn't be," Daniella says.

Outside in these quarters reside a constant portrayal of unscrupulous passing. Night sky bathed in silver. They told each other a lot of things within an hour, remaining with their secrets and desires. Atlases weighing them down around their necks. Great plans being conjured from the wayward trips of these restless souls.

"You still work at that hotel?" John says.

"Only thing I could find up this way. Didn't want to be in the position to choose between freezing or paying rent," Trasc says.

"An undertaking," John says.

"Save us. He's got an idea," Daniella says.

"The grips of it. You all have things going on in your lives. Things that need finishing. Artistic ventures. You young people devote yourselves to each other too quick. You need space to find yourselves. You who are young be happy..."

"Here he goes. Likes to quote things."

"Baby. You can't quote things now lost. Long forgotten."

"No stopping him."

John preserves those words to each their attention. "While you are young let your heart give you the joy in the days of your youth... banish anxiety from your heart and cast off the troubles of your body..."

"Youth is meaningless," Ro says.

"Ah," John smiles looking at her.

"It's all bullshit. Forgot the judgment part. The whole like pillage everything and fear God or fuck everything and burn and war this and everywhere and rape and women suck and property of yours and kill your kids and all that heat."

John smiles at her with a sincere welcoming and understanding and admiration of her rebuttal. "Alright. There's just no joy. You just don't see it."

"John, we can't afford it," Daniella says.

"Nonsense. Back on track here. You have some expansion to be done. New surroundings spark creativity. Get out of the house and divide the sum of a room where my man Adonis keeps. I know how hard it is for you guys to have a place of your own these days. Those in the tight spaces of these ties. A way out. A place to go. We meet back here after some time just like this and share what we've made."

"The place is a bit of a shithole," Trasc says.

John is grinning at his plan and just winks at him. Ro and Lott are fighting amongst themselves about the whole thing. Daniella reluctantly buys in.

"A place to escape the work of this whole drama," John says.

"We need rules," Daniella says.

"Fuck the rules," Lott says. "I ain't got money for this."

"Daniella and I will front most of it. But you need a form of commitment. We always do."

"Should we give blood at the door?" Ro says.

"A sign in sheet to be kept outside the room. There'll need to be some negotiations. Maybe some invites. Rules and limitations. Nothing bound to these governances. No kids allowed."

"He's drunk," Daniella says. "The man drinks two to three bottles a day. That pickled brain of his just about gone afloat."

"Drink wine, save water. You see. I can't think around this negativity. I need this space."

Daniella smacks him. Trasc reaches for a glass of wine but saves his appetite.

"This is about the space we lost out on next door. They'll be coming for this one, too. We don't have the spending luxury we once did. You say no kids, John. You are one," Daniella says.

"I'm sorry about that, Daniella," Ro says.

Daniella smiles and taps Ro's hand across the table.

"No parties. Keep it clean," John says. "You'll have to make some reservations with your other. We should get more people in on this. Spark some debate. Are we the only parents here? Gosh. We are, aren't we?" John says.

"Fuck kids, man," Lott says.

"I think it's like kind of cool you hang with us," Ro says.

"Attachment. What a mess. Come on. This'll be fun," John says. "The things boredom will make us do."

Anxious excitement as they wind down the night with drunken one-sided conversations and mystification of the realms of possibilities to this new game. Everybody just sort of yelling in each other's faces. Nothing fights that were never won. Everything out of context and uninterpreted. Trasc going along for the ride. When the talk becomes dizzying he bows out a moment. Eudora had not partaken in the planning. She trailed off unnoticed and fell asleep out on the lower patio. The only shaded area of the grounds. It seemed to follow her there.

FIFTEEN

The house feels foreign and strange to him. Eudora had another double lined up. He tried to talk her out of it. Daniella told her to take off but she said that she couldn't. They offered and she took it to stay there the night.

When Trasc walked through the door of the empty house he realized what he thought to be withdrawals of some kind having put his drinking off long enough was some kind of panic attack. Thought his heart would stop right there. Actually prepared himself for the end. When the tunnel vision widened and the shortness of breath elongated and the sweat ran cold he was upset with how welcoming he was to it.

It was a new beginning of another end where there was only ever the coming by of things passing. He had felt that he had just about lived his whole life. That things were not going to get any better. He feared the trajectory he and Eudora were heading. He knew there was no way of stopping it.

He tries to ready himself for bed but knows that sleep will not come easy. He has a strong inclination that he's being watched. Doesn't want that to be only because he is tired of being alone.

He sets some weights in front of the door. It wasn't a joke anymore for him. This way of preparation was coming to be a fix of paranoia. He felt his heart breaking his liver rotting and his mind losing. He thought about biting his own tongue off just to stay awake. He set out to making lists. Things he can surprise Eudora with. It felt good making plans for them, even with whatever it is they got themselves into with the mix-up at the hotel.

He looks out in the yard and imagines Eudora out there sunbathing. Pink sky with a hint of blue beyond those paper-mâché clouds. He'd never been more grateful for the lights to come on. To wind down. There is no sound of life. No movement. He lays himself down to rest on the mattress on the bedroom floor barricading the door from the inside. He sleeps with the revolver across his chest. Another revolution to this madness. When did this happen? Thinks about keeping it under the pillow with the barrel pointed up.

The bedroom is small and feels like a coffin. He uses his phone to light his way. It was noticed almost immediately upon checking out the house. Eudora was brave and took everything on the chin. He knew she didn't like the bedroom and he knew she wouldn't like the Ouija board and lone chair sitting up in the attic.

Ghost town therapeutics in the history. He never told her. Told himself throughout the night that the motion sensor out front wasn't behaving in ways in which he could not have it achieve even if he tried. Looking out the peer hole in the front door he thought he saw red smeared in the eyehole. Relieved all the more taking a breath and looking up at the cotton candy sky. He swore there was somebody outside that house.

The attic is right over the bed and he just flat out couldn't sleep like that. Retrieves a lock purchased on the initial supply go ahead for their new digs and installs it on the frame of the door. Eyes swimming. He sets out to complete other things that Eudora needed done around the house. What needed fixing. Surrendering the grand schemes he gives way back to loathing and stillness. It was better that way. He offered himself up for sleep like some migrant on the road taking mud water in fists.

Two front windows to the house and two on the side, one in the bedroom. He was asleep for three hours. You could not walk any which way this terrain without being heard. The trails were carved into woodlands. You so much as breathed and something stirred up beneath you. He could hear animals all through the night.

The trails were used in the settlement days. A lot of powerful people come up this way over time leaving behind ruthless plundering wrapped up inside those chain linked roads. There was a sadness there that was unshakable.

He had taken notes. Gotten information making his rounds. Felt good to be moving. To be working. Excited to share the whispers he's heard with Ford. Most time talking to folks around here they seemed dumfounded by the interaction. Wide-eyed and choking on their own tongues. Like they'd been banished here. Detailed profiles on certain houses and town folk. Was told lots of things he didn't want to hear.

Ford told him that the glitz and glamour of this job was the willingness to lean into the menial and take advantage of people's obliviousness. Could really bog down the stakes of things. Can get boring. Listen to what people were saying, track inconsistencies, and tell yourself a story. Ford had been tailing Trasc before they met but Trasc was different. He noticed.

Heavy footsteps outside the window of the bedroom. He

wakes not because the loudness of them. More because of the pattern and the tempo. Intelligence flooding his being bound by sleep paralysis. Between a place of dream and reality trapped inside of his own skin.

"Is anybody in there?"

It's said outside of the room. Trasc is frozen. He could have sworn he heard the action of a charging bolt. Tries to whittle his breathing down to silent currents. Total absolute stillness. A gray flood between the slits in the curtains the way you can tell the overcast just by certain shades and shadows. Trasc drops between the bed and the wall and trades for his shotgun leaned upright stowed cruiser ready. When he moves it sets off a reaction. Running from outside of the house. Human trampling in retreat.

Out of the bedroom and through the back door he's out and to the side of the house. Tracking footprints in the dirt. Overgrown vegetation grows over a neighboring yard with the abandoned house mere feet away. A window is cracked. Trasc is still in his underwear with the shotgun slung around his shoulder and turns back inside his home.

SIXTEEN

His leg is up and over the window he knocked out when he feels the true ridiculousness of his posturing. The grounds were as if Satan mortgaged a home to grow from the bowels and depths of this incandescent earth. All the insects and wildlife riddling the foliage growing insane in all directions in this private tunneling jungle.

Pieces of the house broke off just by Trasc touching it. Entire shingles of it toppling over. He was a little irritated they didn't just come knock it all down. The town of no light. Despite yellowing dust that hung thick in all directions like paint it remained so that the house was harboring abandoned things left behind. Like only ever these inanimate objects occupied these halls.

Needles and broken glass all over the ground. Plastic pill bottles and tourniquets. There was what looked to be the beginning of a sinkhole. Almost a lean and sway to the house in its entirety. A down below that looked to be just a garbage pile completely dumped atop and filling the lower extremity of the house. A true and very real threat of drowning in that waste.

There was something dead inside. He didn't like the look of it. Wanted to believe it was an animal. Something in him felt sick. He did not feel sick but rather something sickly inside of him that he would need to cut out.

Dropping down into the house from the window is a twelve-foot drop. He crouches when his feet hit the floor. His senses are flooded with whatever dormant and primeval sediments rise from these grounds. He hopes the house will hold for he does not want to be buried with what's in here.

He feels as though he's looking through the veil of some old film reel. Every breath tastes different and has a thickness to it. Feels like he is being exposed to something lethal and damaging. Moving forward takes a certain force to sift through smoke swirls. Enough sickly yellow light shines like bricks embedded into nothing dimming his way. It is as though the surfaces and the raw materials scattered and hoarded around the place project such a light. Like some musty old flea market. Vintage pieces litter the blueprint of the desolation he finds himself standing in. Every step beckons the whole thing to come crashing down.

He slices and pies off the wall. Checking every corner. Movements slow. There is a main room off to the kitchen with a six-pack and a lone chair at the center of it. The chair is positioned looking right off the window he came. Right on towards his house. Trasc kneels and touches the cans and they tell him they have been sitting a while now. Hard to tell either way in the cold.

A lamp with wiring fashioned through the roofing of the place and secured in an electrical socket fitted with a new face panel caging the white bulb runs like veins across the open space. The layout feels like a spiral staircase only it is every floor panel in every room and every wall layered in the whirling of the semblance of experimental architecture.

Fresh coffee grinds dusting counterspace. Wrappers of

protein bars. The under teeth of the kitchen faucet bone dry. He walks on up to a closet in the common space which bleeds into the kitchen. A circling of molded glass with a cross down the center eclipses the room. In the closet are lined clothes of different personages. Doctor, auto-mechanic, gas pump clerk, front desk attendant, tree service, electrician, phone company, jester. An incomplete list. They all look to be the same size.

There looks to be a homemade crate at the bottom of the closet. A perfect square. Trasc kicks it. It's heavy. He lowers to meet it and opens it. Inside are smaller locked boxes. Rolled up blueprints of some kind. As he rifles through he shames himself when his hand meets something dead inside and still warm rocking him backwards.

"Fuck."

Backing away he focuses on the chair in the middle of the room. It wasn't empty. A box with the top left open. Something foregone about it. Trasc steps up to it slowly. It looks to be made and shaped impossibly of stone. Looking inside his mind calibrates what his eyes can see as best the narcoticized and adrenalized system can manage. A large snake with wings attached to it and what looks to be human hair and teeth coiled up over boxes of ammunition and pornographic magazines.

His phone vibrates in his pocket. He steps away. Serpents at his feet. Twin snakes slither by. The neighborhood had an influx of them sometimes run over in mass about the streets. A text from Eudora. She was spending the night with Ro. Lott's night at the loft. Might be staying for drinks at the restaurant and sleeping there. Picked up another shift. In all senses it grounds him and levels his breathing. He takes one final look around the wretched place and makes his way. Two men are walking their dogs when Trasc drops down from the window.

"Hi. My name's Trasc."

The men don't say anything and nothing to calm the dogs who start fighting in the road.

"I live here," Trasc points to his house.

"Okay," one of the men says smiling and waving. He just starts yelling to himself. No other way to put it. The dogs writhing at his feet. He can't stand still. Feet dancing all along the pavement. He smiles at Trasc again and waves. "Hi. Okay. Hi," keeps on yelling.

"Nobody lived in these houses some time now," the other man says. The dogs won't stop barking and snapping. They shift their violences toward Trasc. The man is lax and allows the dogs to maneuver him any which way. "Coyotes got them all wild. Been eating our dogs around here. Them bones up the road there are dog bones. You best be careful now."

The other man starts barking and growling. Howling at the stars behind the veil of daytime sky. Looks down at his phone and grabs at himself. He wasn't the first like this Trasc encountered. Like there was some kind of plague around here. This sort of self-induced debilitating mindlessness. Hard to tell if the man did not speak English or just flat out couldn't. This laced universe of the subhuman willing themselves to metaphysical sicknesses.

"I'm a licensed firearms owner and a rookie PI."

"PI. Right, pal. Me too. You are under investigation. You aren't the only one strapped, hoss. About the only thing most people got going for them. They guns. What were you doing in there?"

"Link to a case I'm working. Had an intruder in the house. Almost certain."

"Almost certain."

"That's right. Jesus. Will you shut them the fuck up."

"Welcome to Hopatcong."

"Love thy neighbor. You know where to find me."

The men walk off and Trasc makes his way into his house and calls Ford. He arrives in less than an hour. Trasc just sips loaded coffee on his stoop as he waits on him and out these shakes. Not a word about the terrain. Not a sound.

"It's a DB," Ford says.

Trasc can smell it on him. "Person?"

"Yeah. A person. A he. As a matter of fact, I don't know what he is. After all these years I still don't know what to make of the dead. I don't want to speak for him. This fucking town. Couldn't tell you how many cases I worked around here over the years. Lot of foul play. Lot of suspect folk. Lot of history."

"Never much good history."

"Nope."

"Don't do that."

"Don't do what?"

"Look around here as much you're doing."

"You're right. It's disrespectful. This ain't your place."

"Fuck you."

"Fucked every which way. You and me and everybody."

"You saw them boxes."

"It's a good find."

"I've been studying. I'm hungry."

"Me too, kid. Starving."

"You know what I mean."

"Yeah. I do. Stay it."

"What do you make of all that in there? Shit I heard?"

"I don't know. I think you're under a lot of stress."

"Stress."

"It kills."

"So does the son of a bitch we should be hunting. When do we start catching?"

"I'll look into it."

"This guy puts our vics in boxes that they make themselves all to prove what? We're all teeth and no heart?"

"That's a way of putting it."

"Anyone prove it?"

"Prove what?"

"The heart part."

"Yes."

Ford walks about the infrastructure of the small house. Starts looking through Trasc's clothes.

"Excuse you," Trasc says. "And your shoes, man. You were just tramping around a DB. This is a Hawaiian household. No shoes."

"You had no strong male role models as a kid. None of yous did."

"Yous."

"Yeah. Yous. Kids. I don't know where to draw the line anymore. When boys become men. Like the fucking kid down the block you're checking in on. This new breed you're saying. Get the hell off your pseudo moralistic high ground. Like you're any different. Start acting like a man, talking like a man, dressing like a man, carrying yourself like a man, showing up like a man. On time."

"How many of you have this complaint when it's time you're running out of. Time you wasted."

"You want to solve things. Fix things. All but your own mess, kiddo. If work was the damn bed you would sleep on the floor."

"I do sleep on the floor. Have slept in worse places."

"You have shit around here that needs fixing."

"You think I don't know that? You know what it's like to have her call her father with me right in the next room because a drill bit won't catch? Makes us feel useless. I'm not meant to be a homeowner."

"Thrice I know all too well. Hard pressed solving a woman's desires."

Ford brushes by Trasc, shouldering him on the way out.

"Get a suit and tie. Call if you need me to put it on you."

Water sloshes under his feet at a centimeter in depth and floods through the crack of the entryway. When he steps outside streams of water are running down both sides of the road. There was no sign of rain at this end where such inundation was to be shared.

SEVENTEEN

Driving down the neck of a bottle right on down these cutthroat roads. Feeling of breaking his own neck just keeping his head upright. Bone tired. A hunger and a thirst intertwined with these antediluvian streets. Ready to cut his own gullet and let the drink pour out.

Swinging through Landing Trasc would scoff at the funeral home that welcomed you into town. An absolutely immaculate building erect this crumbling infrastructure. Like it was there just a sort of factory seeing everybody to and from this place. It looked like the only thing with power in town. The only other stable structures were unkept and unattended but pitstops and the Liquor Factories. Like nobody was meant to stay here.

To get him through the night Trasc broke from his brief tradition of sobriety. Bottles jangling next to him. Sit upright very much his passenger. Not a soul in his vision. A dark that his headlights cannot vanquish. The night pushing back the rays. Considers flipping on the windshield wipers to combat the waves of light reflecting off all this blackness. Not a hubris take but the very nature of his surroundings. The Hopatcong dark could be the place entire. The weather and the company. He drives slow.

There was a long gravel road that once he hit he knew he was homeward bound. Built in get home paths stored in memory. Something that came back little by little when the drinking stopped. The cell service couldn't be trusted out here.

Long, narrow, beaten path. The vehicle would elevate in ways he thought to be impossible physics. The exhaust choking on fumes. Gears gone mad. There was no level ground here. No safe space.

He often thought about riding these waves with is hands up. Hit the lights and drive straight into the brick wall bordering a house at the corner. A left there at the end of the road right up on that wall. Down another road and a right then down that road and he was just about home. Making the simple left at that last house was like parallel parking at the edge of a canyon.

All his addictions started to fester. The shame coming about. This long stretch of road was about a mile and a half long. A mile to go. Rough shape way starting to wear beneath him. Potholes the size of craters with nearly impassable mud pits. Every few seconds he thought it to be the last of the old vehicle as something slammed up underneath it and tore away. None of this mattered. He was soaring.

The mile becoming a millisecond. He worried about this road. This long and slow road toward such a desperate and tragic Roman death that came too soon but never soon enough. There were tears in his eyes. He tried to regain when that started to happen and just what would go through his mind at the end of this voyage. Houses tightly tucked away like sores all around him. Nothing level but this straight road. Not even his life. None other than this hold to an end. He grips the steering wheel and picks up speed and screams as the wall comes into focus and a greater light is let to be. He slams on the breaks.

He's at the corner right up on the wall. Beyond that a house perched up in silence. To his left nothing but the light and the rumbling of a truck engine. Trasc looks out his window with a hand over his eyes. Lowers the window and waves the vehicle along. He'd need to back out and pull into a driveway for them to fit. Most of the houses didn't have one or the space. He wouldn't be on down the way he needed if the truck didn't do the same. There was a patch of land leading into the trails right of the truck.

"Hey. Better yet. Pivot right up there and I'll make my way through," Trasc says.

Nothing from the driver of the truck. Harassing engine chugging along.

Trasc remains shielding his eyes. It wasn't far off from parking inside the sun. He laughs. A friendly gesture. He can make nothing out of the light save for its mercy. Its grace.

"Bit of a pickle. I got nowhere to go, buddy. Let me see if I can squeeze through."

Nothing.

Trasc taps at his horn.

"Come on, partner."

The engine ceases but the lights remain. Trasc can't see a thing but he can hear and it'd been happening all too quickly. Dead quiet desolation. A door opens to the truck and heavy boots thud to the ground. He can no longer investigate the light without it being deafening. Not blinding but deafening. Something sharp in the head. The door shuts and there's what Trasc knows to be the charging of a rifle. Trasc dives into the passenger seat.

A storm of steel. Dry times, prayers for rain, it comes in brass. Shells lashing down. The loss of hearing is immediate. Magazines emptying. The man reloading with great speed.

The lights go out but the muzzle flash from the barrel in synchronicity with the automatic bursts do just fine lighting flares of pitilessness. Trasc presses himself as far down into the car as he can reaching for the passenger side door.

His entire being convulses. He can't reach the handle. The revolver was in the glovebox and he grabs it. Has a split second to aim and fire. Doesn't trust the trajectory of the shot. The bulleted percussion picks up in rampant, unrelenting succession.

Trasc gets the passenger side door open and crashes atop broken glass and concrete. The bottles followed him on the way down. Save for the bottles that just might be all there was in terms of glass. He's frantic for cover. Sits back on a tire. Crawls over to the next. Logic was low in the high emotions. All there was to do was to keep moving. The man is reloading and Trasc draws for another shot, praying for his aim to be true, and he takes it.

Light primer strike.

Trasc takes cover. Works at his weapon. Hunched and bowed and unsteady hands in prayer for his demise. Machine gun fire in numbing havoc. It has taken hold and shape of that very light. Silent and all blistering. Trasc pans left then right then left again.

Nothing was hitting the vehicle. No glass. No smell of oil or gasoline. Unscathed metal. Nothing traveling by with promise of impending doom but the dread within the godlessness of the moment.

The gunfire comes to a halt. Trasc's head booming. Everything muffled. The door to the truck opens and closes. He didn't hear the engine starting up again. Just sees the lights peeling away. Caliginous sifting about leaden in a pool underfoot. Plumes of unicellular smoke floating by like blackholes about the barony of the sleeping and the living. His breath shakes within and without him. Salt and gunpowder on his tongue. The thought of those fallen vital about this sequence gets him to his feet.

He takes out his phone keeping his eyes forward as he rounds about his vehicle keeping the revolver raised at retention. No service. He flicks the flashlight on. It only intensifies the fumigating insubstantiality of reek moonshine. The truck was cut and righted for safe passage roaring on down the road the opposite way. Trasc breaks in a dead run for it. Something trips him up. Concrete welcoming him. Bludgeoning him. He rolls on his back breathing hard looking up at the starless sky as augury and listens to the truck's tires rigid and grim escaping into the contours. Shells grating on the ground with every movement. The man was shooting blanks.

Left behind and what tripped him up is a small wooden box. Trasc gets to his feet. Steps through the brassy pond. Crouches down and shines the phone light on it. Small paper left behind. Eyes scaling the page.

'Many words mark the speech of a fool... slow to speak... bite your tongue... everything meaningless, chasing the wind, nothing gained under the sun... lay waste the earth... valleys of slaughter... the tongue is also on fire... haughty eyes, a lying tongue, and hands that shed innocent blood... the perverse tongue will be cut off...'

Trasc folds the paper and puts it in his pocket. Puts his hands on his hips and looks around him. No dead. Nobody at all. Not a sound but the drone of mosquitoes and other beasts with wings. His phone dies and the last light goes out. He bends down and opens the box and cannot see so much inside as but the shape of a small thing the size of a stone. His hand shakes as he reaches inside. Picks it up at the fingertips. Swollen, gelatinous, dry, coarse. He thinks it to be a slug of some kind and holds it up to the sky and sees what it is and tosses it falling back and moving away from the box. Then he just sits there with his head in his knees.

He gets up and moves over to the broken bottles at the side of his car and drops down to his knees before the broken glass. Presses his palms down into it and brings it to his lips and his nose. Wants to press his lips up to the booze left in the street and suck it dry. It could have been blood spilt to him. He drops down once more. Immobilized and sweating in the gloom.

He didn't know what was more unbelievable. What just happened. Or the fact nobody has stepped out of their homes to see what did.

EIGHTEEN

John is driving home from Mal's field hockey game when he comes up on the burning church. Chaos at the home. Daniella grew increasingly against taking part in the hotel. Mal told her what John said. Tag that along with John telling her to take this and run with it. How she was always too distracted at the house or the restaurant to get anything done for herself. He was not welcome at the game but she'd been giving it a shot. John went and stayed off to the side. Thought about if maybe they'd had a bigger problem than they liked to admit for a while now.

Black smoke rising in the distance as he nears. He's praying when traffic takes him all the way through to the scene. He didn't know what to make of that.

He pulls over and gets up on it as closely as the crowd permits. He heard about these sorts of things ramping up. People shepherding the end times in with a rave. Wondered who in this gathering came from one of the tent cities. Rumors of proprietors funding these sorts of events. He could always tell where people were plugged into.

He'd never been in a protest. Hard for him to think of it as such. He's swept up into the crowd walking amongst them. He starts to make familiar faces from the game. Then he sees his own. Sees Mal. Clear skies despite the smoke. She stands with a torch next to a boy in a hood. Dubstep and airhorns blaring.

"What the fuck is this?" John is on them. He takes the torch and stomps it out and pushes the kid against a light pole by the throat. "Look me in the eyes, boy. See the hood in them. I'm the authentic version of the front you'd always been putting up. You go and help put the fire out. GO."

"Dad," Mal says.

"You were baptized here."

"I know. Just…"

"Go home."

"But…"

"NOW, MAL. Take my car."

It wasn't a tough commute. The Circle right across the road. Some kids are trying to set a large processional cross on fire. Christ's sad eyes projects through all the mayhem. John can't help but make contact with them. Seems a thing needing to be saved.

John walks towards the kids and they see something in his stride they don't like and walk off. Firetrucks arrive on the scene combating the vicious swells of the building. John knows most of the volunteers personally. He watches Mal drive off and acts on reactionary accounts alone. John begins to drag the cross.

He tucks his arms underneath the cross and stagger steps backwards. When his hamstrings give out he turns and props the cross upon his back and hammers forward one heavy trodden step after the next, focusing on his breathing. He's sweating but soon enough he is clear of the church compound and the heat leaves him like a great weight, lessening the enormity of mass he carries. He trudges on.

Into the neighborhood and down the way to the Circle. He stumbles and falls. Rights himself, rises, continues on. His nails break. He busts a lip and chews a piece of his cheek off as he grinds his teeth. His cardio wasn't the best, but he still had his brawn. Brute strength and rage over technique. Nothing pretty about this. Skin breaks and he feels it all about him in the cold like a tearing.

He starts crying. The source comes upon him like something unknown yet strangely familiar. Like an all too great weight lifted. The feeling of something the likes of an embrace. Chills and goosebumps run down his person. There was nothing beautiful about this place and so he'd been forced to find it in his mind's eye. The weather stayed the same. People never changed or grew. There was no color but the strangeness of the houses. He can't help but find his baby girl behind the veil of his very own head. He thinks about that and about carrying the son of a bitch who took her away from him. She'd made a cliché of him. Felt like he was being punished.

Oh, heavenly Father. The blood on my hands is not near the blood you spilt by the hands of sinners for sinners to gift us the merit of the day and this luxury of our lives. The blood my baby girl spilt is on you. You're the sinner.

John drops down in the middle of the street with cries of reverie. People come out of their homes to help him carry the cross. Neighbors he knows. Faces he sees but knows not their names. His own name is called out from porches, stoops, steps. Brothers and sisters a part of this human family running to his side. Their proud leader, fallen. Lifting he and Him up, up, and away. Down the road and planted on John's yard.

"John?" Daniella says. She's at the door bathed in porch light.

John is ruined and wet and cold on the lawn breathing

hard over the cross. He looks at the cross and at his wife then back to the cross again. Looks on down the road at the black on black plumes relentlessly taking to the stars. Throws his hands up and just keeps on shaking his head and repeating. Then nothing but weeping.

"I don't know. I don't know, baby. Oh, God. I don't know... I don't know... I don't know I don't know..."

Daniella holds her husband in their yard. Let's him feel weak, afraid, and small.

"You don't need to know anything, my beautiful man. My king. You just need to care."

NINETEEN

Eudora stands in the hot shower in the dark until it goes cold. She was always weary about things such as water usage. Recycling and using clean materials. Lately she'd just been throwing everything in the same garbage bin. Her way of life has become completely and totally disposable.

The sensation of the hot water hits her in ways a first beer would after a brief hiatus from the sauce. Her father had done good work in the house. Made her a lightweight and she felt temporarily lightheaded consumed within the steam. She has not seen another human face on these two days off. It filled her with such a defiling dread that she didn't know what to do with herself. Spent most of the day asleep on the couch with bedsheets on the windows because the sun only made her feel condemned and guilty. Trasc would rub her feet or her shoulders on days like this. She was still sore from the stretch of days. The hot water soothed her neck and traps. She closes her eyes and imagines the water as fingertips rolling down her shoulders. She had lost the desire for the sensation of contact or touch elsewhere. So young and dried up already. She'd been losing weight and probably now barely broke a hundred pounds.

Scrolling through social media made her bout with nausea and she put it away. There were reverberations of filling the time with something in all that scrolling that left a panning aftereffect scaling the room. Own sense of isolating apprehension to where she looked unflinching. Left alone her days have become meaningless. Nice days in terms of weather became cross and she resented them. If sunlight through the shades woke her up from a sleep that rarely came she would wake in a jump scare by the mere tenacity of its false promises. The days were beginning to feel like something assigned to her. A body clothed in festering skin. She feared the moment she'd need to rise.

She thought about going to school again. Being around that kind of thing made her nervous. She'd be made to speak. If she were meant to take part in making words she'd take it as some sort of attack on her personally. She let it be known that she'd detested such obligatory demands. What it would take to galvanize herself to seem interested. She was beginning to fall out of comprehension. Failed in seeing her life beyond thirty. There were no such possibilities of sustainability emotionally, physically, kinesthetically.

There was something that would bring about an awful taste in her mouth about every five minutes reminding her of the minutes passing and the minutes to come. The past was present and forever. There was no talking or means of valuable communication. An inability to move on from the worst. To hear anything about it. She knew she would not always be happy but in so she was never happy and it was not out of any rebellion other than trying to climb out of this for the sake of other's around her. She could not appreciate flaws. When she tried to she would pick out three others. She thought about getting an animal. Just as her value to people she didn't think she would be much of use to the thing. A soft train call in the distance. There is nothing to the day but brightness. She sticks to the obscurity of the indoors.

She had it planned and journaled to herself something she had seen by chance. It was an article.

Nine simple ways to show love to yourself today.

Her own words that she writes herself have become deaf and dumb. They no longer held any truth in their claims and it only continued her torture. Her circumstance was in a continual change but not her mindset. Only that of a darkening.

In the article it spoke on the importance of things Eudora had already come to find futile. Finding inner peace. Being of sound heart and mind and dealing with anger and grief. The feeling of being overwhelmed. Climbing out and making sense of this suffering. Leading with positivity and understanding and forgiveness, most of all forgiving yourself. None of it moved her. But she thought she would give it a shot. She had nothing else to do and thought so desperately that it might fill up her day so that finally she would be able to enter sleep world. It is what she'd been dubbing it lately, laughing to herself about it. Dreams were becoming more vivid and she began to fall in love with the people within them. It was sleep that had become the best part of her day. She doubled down on that. Said why not death.

The plan was to take herself out on a date, buy herself some flowers. Dance wild, free, and nude to a playlist made that day. All she could relate to were sad songs. She wanted to wear something that was not pajamas or the black drags she wore for work. She had purchased herself a feast to make. Make a list of things that were and were not working in her life, trying some affirmations to repeat to herself. Break a sweat and move herself like it was something to be maintained. Revisit a favorite movie from old and read something new. Go to the store and pick out a new book and take her time with it.

Sitting and doing none of the self-made plans. Finding the worthlessness in them today that they held yesterday and would possess tomorrow. Eudora daydreamt instead on pumping herself full of dopamine, oxytocin, endorphin, serotonin. See what sticks. These things were airborne only so that they took to the atmosphere and just kept on floating away as tangible things that would be obtained here. She wanted to take the syringe and pump herself full of what they give the sick dog. What a way to go out. She'd only been choking on the fumes of gaslighting herself.

TWENTY

Lott told Ro that he tried to kill himself his third night at the
hotel. Ro was pregnant and she had told him. The
information came on him like this lucid winter that seemed
to bring only intense refulgency and cold. Contradictory
elements to the world in their wandering.

Indoors beckoned movement. Felt awful in sedentary
states. They took Daniella's dog for a walk out in a nature
cleanse. She usually kept the dog at the restaurant. Hoped to
clear Lott's head. The sun sits high and too small to be so
bright. It sat like a split headache in this panorama. He didn't
know what to do with himself coming by such information,
integrating himself with his own infirmity.

Two striking cops were at the bar of the hotel. They got
on him still thinking they were cops. Kept talking about race
traitor this and race traitor that in the room they kept. Lott
didn't know who he was talking about. He thought the whole
idea was stupid. Didn't understand it. Took her bosses to be
the privileged type who did these sorts of things just to do
them. They never went around much. The room had
nothing uplifting about it. The drugs wouldn't bring him

down and he had a bad episode. Didn't know what to do with himself and thought the cops were waiting for him outside the room.

A few times he arrived at the hotel there was somebody out from tent city inside the room. That shady ass landlord who ran things over there would come with some of his boys and drag them off. Look Lott up and down and inside the room like they knew all that was going on inside and wanted something in there. Smiled like they'd be coming to take it.

Lott never told Ro he fucked one of the tent city folk for some cash the last time he'd gone up. He felt a tremendous amount of lacking in his remorse or guilt. Hadn't thought about it or her since. He concocted a story and told himself that was why they had gotten this place. To indulge in these impossible desires that we try so desperately to curb with over the counter truths and meanings that create only more boundaries until one must commit great massacres inside. He leaned into the inception of this whole relationship shebang not being such a road without turns.

We were made to believe we would be satisfied with one single person in the eternity of our lives. It seemed ridiculous to him even at an early age. There was a bit of hush-hush to the whole deal. Don't kiss and tell. He didn't think we were meant for such bonds. That we do it out of an impulse to be hoarders of people. To vanquish any sense of this aloneness sitting unconquered in a corner of ourselves.

"You should have called me," Ro says.

"I'm no good for you. For a kid. You'd be better off."

She smacks him and keeps on hitting him. "Don't say that. You don't get to decide."

"It's the truth."

"We don't fly together, baby. We fall beautifully. Make like snowflakes. Not one is the same, right? We aren't like everybody else. Don't live by their limitations. Their rules.

We would raise them up good. I'll pick up more shifts until I can't anymore. This'll be fun."

"We are getting married. Having a kid…"

"What you saying?"

"I need to be better."

"Married?"

"That's right."

"You proposing?"

"Maybe."

"Okay."

"You all have been using this time to work on yourselves. Working on your shit. Your videos. I never been able to go to school. I can treat this like my master class, you know what I'm saying? Read those pop books and shit."

"You make an obvious liar out of yourself. I can't think straight these days. You said you'd work on your art. Review vids taking off. My channel has so much traffic. It feels good when you get stuff done," she told him her great plans to fortify her belief in them. "I made so much content the other night."

Comfort in the distance between them and the industrial world. They took turns carrying the dog after about fifteen miles in. They had simply gotten lost and laughed when the dog stopped and turned over on his side. Caring for the dog she saw something change in Lott's cruelty. They stop and eat in silence and sit in it for some time.

"I'm sorry, Ro. For everything. So fucking sorry."

"No rule book on how to do this."

Sirens in the distance.

"We should leave. Going to get dark soon," Ro says.

"How long we going to carry him?"

"As long as I've carried you. Let's go."

They walk on through the darkening woods. Wild sounds howling through the night. The trees are bare and skeletal like rising oak bars of this arcadian prison, trapping them inside. They're locked in as they move into a clearing and find the box. It stands tall and spray painted white. The size of a two-car garage. Red writing on one of the walls.

SKIN FOR SKIN. A MAN WILL GIVE ALL HE HAS FOR HIS OWN LIFE.

A body inside that they can neither tell male or female. They're all chewed up and bleeding out badly. White eyes on the entrance as Ro and Lott turned the corner fading away. It's almost as if they're smiling. They can see teeth marks in the abdomen. Muttering a few last words.

"I'm fine. I'm fine. I'm fine..."

TWENTY-ONE

Trasc was coming up the road with supplies to work on the house with Rich when he saw the car parked right up on the fence of the front yard. Eudora pulling more doubles. They've been avoiding one another, he knew this. Avoided that truth, too. He hadn't told anybody about the other night but Ford. Kept the shotgun on him at all times since.

The road had to clear itself from his field of vision as it rises up to him like a slow cart on a track. Registry of information within him fumbling around in the dark. Before him are revelations only made by single beads of brail amongst the scorched landscape that he had to reach out to touch blinded by the white, cold heat. Bright day, almost a violence to it, bringing about no clarity. He knows the car Rich drives and it's not his.

A man is running from the house. He's wearing a medical mask that covers his face and dark sunglasses. As Trasc pulls into his driveway the man gets into the car. He doesn't drive away.

Trasc gets out of his car and looks at the house then back

to the car again. Moves around to the driver side door and taps on the glass. Places a hand on the weapon in his pocket.

"Buddy. Can I help you?"

"I'm sorry," he's of small frame and he doesn't look at Trasc. Only cracks his window. Locks the vehicle.

"What were you running from?"

"To my car."

"Yeah. Right. You were running from my house."

"It's not your house."

"What?"

There is only time for a brief struggle. Trasc tries to slip an arm through the window. The man rolls up the window and drives away. His eyes can't make the plates and he felt inferior about that. Trasc was about to start up the road.

"Adonis."

Turns to find Rich pulling up behind him.

"Who was that?"

"Nobody."

———

The old man was running circles around him. Trasc couldn't keep up. He figured it would wind up this way and went shopping. Mainly because he was getting low on booze and low financially, but that never stopped him. There was nobody responsible in that regard. Nobody around to stop him. He stole most of his loot anyway. Started feeling useless around the house and that never quit. He wore his own futility like a coronet.

Coffee and breakfast sandwiches. Taylor ham egg and cheese. Trasc had a bad nose, but he could imagine something like burnt swine. He stays fasted. Heightened his focus. Didn't like eating out. Liked feeling light and in a haze throughout the day. Stuck in a nervous state of sweating out the oblivions of the night prior only to repeat in ignorant arrogance the next. Each morning was something of a resurrection through migraines and stomach pains. He was a professional about it and a tyrant to himself. Figured the less he ate the quicker he'd get drunk. He could go hungry but not sober.

Rich eats both sandwiches. He kills a coffee, cracks a beer, and lights a cigarette. He had left these things behind a time before Trasc met him. Hadn't realized Rich took smoking up again.

While Rich was fixing things up Trasc hangs photographs he'd taken around the neighborhood on long walks getting a lay of the land. Considered it work. Ford told him to draw timelines. Looking for inconsistencies. Detecting. Discrepancies that led to curiosities. Disturbances in the abstractions of the world that commandeered the concrete, discursive realities an investigator should look for. It was starting to settle in. Pick things up and put them down. It wasn't anything but insufficiency.

"Eudora working?"

"Yep."

"She's a hard worker."

"Learned it from you."

"Let's hope that's all she's learned."

"You ain't that bad."

"Things considering."

"We fuck up, Rich. You and Eudora have gotten a lot better. Guys stopped talking about damn politics. Could finally learn something about her. There's a lot to like."

"Yeah."

"You and me have gotten a lot better, too."

"Nothing much to like there."

Trasc laughs it off. It was nice, the stillness about this.

Rich regards the wind as something blowing with irritability. The way that it funneled down into the place.

"Fifteen minutes away and you would think I went to the other side of the moon. I don't think I have ever seen a blue sky here. I'll drive out and be hit with clarity on the main road," Rich says. "All these years and I never come up this way before."

Trasc seldom spoke to anyone these days face to face. Eudora had a way about her of finding ways of getting distracted. Moving about frantically even if she was listening to you from inside a jail cell. There are services requiring payment for listening. It left nothing but transactional speech. She had a mode of being somewhere between sleeping and being strung up by her hair. It was a good thing it would all be coming to an end of all things come to pass. He sometimes was afraid she'd never get any rest and she'd run herself right into the ground straight to hell. The ending was its own healing. He felt grateful for her. He had seen the terrible memories that reside in the old in all of Rich's irritabilities.

"Good to get out of the house," Rich says.

"Not working?"

"Winter. Ground is too hard. I don't know what to do with myself."

"Lot of that going around. How's the old lady?"

"Not good."

"How long have you been married?"

"Something like thirty years."

"You can try the hotel."

"What the hell am I going to do in there? You all are lucky having those given gifts to you. Something to fill the time."

"They don't feel like gifts. You got to like what you do or you wouldn't do it."

"That's how it works. We do what we do not want to do or what we are forced to do. There's no middle ground."

"You're good at it."

"Breaking my back?"

"Breaking my balls."

"Yeah. Why's the hell you can't do anything."

"Anything?"

"With your hands. A man has got to use his hands."

"We use them for different things."

"Your writing?"

"Yes."

"That ain't work."

"Happy to hear you feel that way."

"A man's got hands. You can have brains. Got yourself a pair. Size and strength and talent. But a man has hands," Rich grabs Trasc by the wrist and squeezes so hard that he feels it in his teeth. "Feel what I can do with these hands? Them are some man hands. You let them get idle and that's the end of that. You have girl hands, man. A thin neck."

"These are my money makers," Trasc wiggles spirit fingers. "Don't make me start walking around like Curley."

"I read that book," Rich's eyes widen with excitement.

"That's the one. The plan was to maybe read another one after it."

"Hurts my head."

"Got nothing in there to hurt. It would be the only politics you need. We hold God's feet to the flame."

"How much money you making? With the writing."

"You see my car over there that your wife can't drive no more? The house here your daughter pays for. The phone in my pocket mind you, too. These one pair of boots and these one pair of jeans living. Safe to say about that much, Rich. I can make more money mowing the lawn in my underwear and videotaping it. Nobody reads anymore."

"Pick up a trade. Learn something."

"I ain't saying I can quit it. You can't walk out on it that easily."

"Writing?"

"Obsessions."

"I never wanted to be anything."

"You're decent. Honorable. Noble. You provide in ways I don't. Can't."

"I think you're hard on yourself."

"Tough space between the ears. Own worst critic."

"You all are pretty hard tough on yourselves. Young people."

"We need to be. World makes us that we need to be."

"I see a great loneliness."

"Damn, Rich. A great loneliness. There's a poet in you yet."

"You shown me there ain't much difference between what me and you do. But I can't learn what you got. You got to learn."

"Eudora…"

"I'm dying."

"What?"

"You heard it."

"Jesus, Rich."

"Don't bother. I never talked to the man in my life. He don't want to hear it."

"What the hell you doing about it?"

"Just told you. Dying."

"That isn't doing anything but quitting."

"Got me thinking it just might be the only doing I ever done."

"Why do you say that? Talk like that? You know how many times you have devalued life in front of her? How do you imagine that makes her feel? When we all get together and everybody looks so damn miserable. Can't even fake it. Did you think that your portrayal of suffering would somehow go unnoticed. That you were somehow unloved in such ways that nobody would care about this worldview? You can't die. If you die she'll die. I know it."

There's something in Rich's eyes he's never seen much of. Little magnitude for compassion or sentimentality inside those craters. There is plenty of shade in the yard. Murky blockades presenting such as walls. Where shadows lay the wind does not move and it silences everything and makes it all very still. He can see the wetness in Rich's eyes move about in breathtaking rivulets. Never noticed how blue and clear and full of life they still were. He sees Eudora's eyes within them. He can hear him bottling up something much more vulnerable inside of his throat and chest.

"She needs you. You don't want to admit that," Trasc says.

"Take better care of her, Adonis. You need to learn. You're not stupid. You're lazy. And you're a liar."

Trasc lets Rich have the final say. Has nothing to say his own self. Rich gets up and thinks twice before tossing the remnants of his sandwich out over to the abandoned house. Bear country. Mouths what's left and looks up at the sun and then at the house. Takes in a deep breath through the nose.

"It's a nice house. It just needs work."

"Good thing you'll be around."

Rich pulls out another beer as if from some hidden utility from about his person. Cracks it open and sips it. Smacks his lips. He opens the gate but before he steps out he stops and turns to Trasc.

"I see it. Parents know these things."

"What?"

"The change in her. Her... declining. I can't recognize her week to week sometimes."

"I know."

"She never shows it. You seen me lighten up on her. Why do you think?"

"I know."

"Why do you think?"

"I know."

"She would say I love you. I would call her sometimes. I do call her sometimes. I don't know why. I don't know why I just worry about her. Like I just sense this terrible thing. That's got to be genealogy or something. I think it's hard to not notice. She would say I love you and I would never say it back. Why? Why would I never say it back?"

"You can call her and tell her now, Rich."

TWENTY-TWO

She woke in the empty house on what would be her final day on her birthday cursing the day. Not a single regard from anybody. Her mother had called.

"Hello."

"Hello."

"Mom."

"Who is this?"

"Mom. It's me."

"Bitch. You bitch."

"Okay."

"I don't know what happened to you. You've changed. No daughter of mine."

"It's my birthday."

"Hello. Who is this? Hello."

"Okay. Bye, mom. I love you."

Trasc promised big plans but took it he drank all the way through his shift at the hotel and slept there. She wanted to skip the whole obligation of giving it any mind. Early and just having tossed and turned away the night she felt tired beyond all reckoning. As though she's been alive for a hundred years.

It is a beautiful day and this registers in the manner this world sometimes imbues by just the sounds of it. Birdsong a mere decoy and trap to the magnet drawing card of false allurement to the snare of coming days. She slept with the window open and the shades tied.

She and Trasc were keeping superiorly different schedules. Never slept together. Rarely woke together. He had been working on something and stalled and she had hoped the move might spark something. Told him to take this time between work and write and not to worry about anything. Despite what he would think, she'd been thinking about him all along. The house would be perfect. Set him up. He'd be okay. She puts the cash she'd been stowing away for him in an envelope and tapes it to the kitchen table with a final letter. She would not be without means and efforts of survival.

Malachi is in the passenger seat. She had given the key to Ja. They were driving holding hands listening to her father's new album. He wrote and produced it at the hotel. Something about the room and the isolation bringing about inspiration. A song at the end of it for her sister.

"We used to get our food from this farm we had," Mal says looking at her reflection in the glass. Traces the stars in the night sky flooding her outline. Considers herself a ghost with a belly full of constellations. "My dad would forcefully inseminate the cows and keep them in this small, steel box. Take their kid and butcher it and he would do this over and over again to the same cow. They'd cry all night long. Horrible sounds. I hated him for it. I want to do something with animals, I think. I think we can change the world. You know what I mean?"

Ja turns the music up and drives into the night. They pull up to a tent city on the outskirts of the hotel. There's a guy strung up on a cross stripped and battered right upon entering the slums. A man in a white suit sits on the side of it counting money. Ja grabs Mal's hand and tries to hurry by him.

"You going to pay or wind up on my T, Lil J buddy."

"Fuck you, Micah."

"Your girl. She'll just get the D."

Two men step before them but Micah waves them off.

"Welcome home. Just cause you family don't mean you don't owe. Everybody owes," Micah says.

They keep moving. There's no formation about them. No community. Some of them don't even have tents. Just sleeping in trash bags. The spines of men and women bent and out of shape. Nobody on their feet. Everybody huddled over a screen. There is no solid ground to stand upon. All of it just muck and filth. A small child building mud castles and covered in the stuff looks up at them with glass in her hair. They move on.

Mal tries to find some nature around the exterior. It creates a barrier of all its callings and trappings. There's a mesh of rap and heavy metal music. People don't have shoes, but they have phones. There doesn't seem to be water but there are bottles of other substances. Orange and glass. Brown and clear. Syringes and needles and spoons.

The place sits in its gravitational territorial occupation perfectly cut and molded into its quarters of depravity. There are no natural passages, entries, or exits to the naked eye. A beautiful, confusing, and harsh terrain, however barren. A community in trash and hardship. Fascinating in its medieval port, undeniable in its scale, yet utterly claustrophobic. The ghetto spins and Mal is ready for sleep. Wanted to just go to the hotel and watch movies. Break the rules further and invite some friends. Ja wanted to get high and fuck.

Nowhere she looks or turns does nature above her bend or twist the same way or the right way. Not a tree in view. Nothing that grows. In the night, pockets of empty space are shaded differently. Like some other tent of some other fabric of some other dark that one can just lie down in and die. The savage encapsulation of it all is ravaging.

"You want some?" a man says. "You want some. I got some."

Ja sees to the man sitting in front of his tent. He grips Mal's hand tightly. She's been trying to pull him in the opposite direction. He has a deck of cards in hand. Some men and women roll dice nearby. Bystanders spread around sporadically. Some among them are in masks.

"Right on, right on. Listen here," the man shuffles the deck, "you're alright by me. Just as long as you give me the right toward what you're packing. All you got. A fair and even shake. We got something planned, you see. Something big. I know the story. Your story. We don't keep secrets," the man says. "Nah, man. Big plans. We all tired of you thinking you're better than us round here. I'm talking to you, girl. I see you around here with J baby," gets up and steps in Mal's way. Ja pushes him to the ground.

"Sit your ass down," Ja says. "Punk ass. Let's play. What you got."

"Oh, I got. I got a lot."

"Why you hounding her, Phez. Leave her be," another man says. Speaking shadows. He pulls on a wine bottle. "Yeah. She really lightens up the place."

"What's your stake?" Phez says.

"What you got all in in the middle. Hold'em," Ja says.

"Texas. I like it. Been meaning to head down that way."

"You ain't going shit."

"Keep talking shit."

"Fuck you. You got or not. You play or we dip."

"Bet. Bet. Just having a conversation is all. Never much for parties. The spoils are nice. The not working is nice. I embrace my laziness. My uncanny, uniquely, lovely urgency and proficiency to rot. Never could figure out what to do with all this time, I'm saying. Figured out the art of wasting it. I got a knack for devouring hours. I like this place, I do. Nothing ever changes. And we keep no time."

"Phez. Nobody wants to hear your crap," another man says. "Let the boy swing for the sky. He wants to get high and high and high."

Mal lets it play out. Getting a read and a feel. She stands tall, shoulders back, and unintimidated. This place does not unsettle her. It feels strangely familiar. Strangely like home.

"Shut the fuck up," Phez says. "Shit, he's just sorry he's got the attention span of a gnat. They all do. I'm something of the one who runs this town, you see, girly. Just setting the tone here. Vibing with our new friend. Think of me as your welcoming mat. In this place, time is forgotten. Ja might not have given you the skinny. Matter of fact. I tried to bounce," Phez puts some pills in the middle of the table and starts shuffling the deck. Sets some poker chips down and motions for Ja to take a seat. Winks at Mal as he hits a joint.

"Talk to yourself," Ja sits down with his eyes on the drugs.

Phez spits in his hand and slaps it on the table. "Wound up right back here. Like this is all there'll ever be. All there is."

"Deal the fucking cards, man," Ja says.

"Could just fight for it. Give these cats a real show."

"Been there done that. You a pussy, Phez."

"Mhm. I love the smell of pussy," Phez smells the air eying Mal.

"I ain't repeating myself. We make this fast. Short stack."

Mal didn't take the wager seriously. Nothing shaken upon, nothing signed. A few hands in Ja has Phez beat. A small crowd around them. Phez is just laughing in his fists as Ja rakes in the pills and the chips with the last hand on the table. Phez draws a pistol and points it right at Ja's face.

"You think you cheat me and walk up on out of here?"

"You lost, bitch. Like you always do. All you know how to do, Phez."

"Nah, man. I see what you did. I see it."

A man standing over Phez holds a knife to his throat.

"Ain't losing this place. Got kids here. Put the gun down."

"Who come take it," Phez laughs. "You tell me. Huh? The fuck the consequence?"

"Somebody always come knocking. This is my home now. Put the gun down, Phez. Not tonight. Not here."

Phez drops the gun and pushes everything on the table towards Ja and off the table and into his lap then flips the table and stands.

"Yeah. Not tonight. Not here. I know what y'all be doing. Fucking folks like you. Run the world run right up into the ground," Phez says.

Ja gathers his loot and grabs Mal's hand and pushes her along.

"Mhm. Not tonight. Not here. I'll be seeing you," Phez says blowing kisses at them.

They turn and walk off. Trudging on they pass a small field akin to farmland with children at work. They tend and wrestle the cold dead soil, backs breaking with hoes larger and heavier than their own insular being condemned to this labor. They all wear masks of some kind. Unearthly plague doctors stepping out of hell and into another, digging mass graves. There is a pale horse standing warden to it all. Starved and far too thin and shackled. Ja tells Mal not to look back. She could see nothing ahead. Heavy, cold rain falling. Micah bidding them farewell.

TWENTY-FOUR

Trasc drove into the hotel with two bottles of wine on him. He was working overnight folding laundry. Pulled one or two nights a week as a transfer just to keep three digits in the bank. He drank one on the job with his laptop setup on laundry bins. Planned on doubling down in the room and by then would need another. He would park as far as he could so that he would be able to get steps in. Drinking the night prior he would have been asleep most of the day. He was regimented about it and totally critical in arranging his days around drinking. He was in complete control of eviscerating himself. He worked on becoming a better detective. It sounded silly at first but he started getting very serious about it. Walking around a room talking to himself trying to forge concrete meaning to things became routine. Working the desk overnight he shut the place down to his liking and began working cases both his own and as a sort of mental exercise. Ford gave him files on Boxman. Before he gets out of the car he takes a pill and hits two shooters and chases it with coconut water from an actual coconut he got from a woman in tent city. Then he just sits there looking out at the gleaming night listening to the sad sounds of it all. Cars trespassing on highways lead to nowhere. All about canvassing everything they leave behind red lights transposed and sifting in a silent hue of red dark. It was blistering cold and the overlooking lot adjacent to the building was absolutely covered in black ice. Nothing but cold and dark and weight. Not a light on him. Boots that give no proper footing. He walked the whole way almost becoming stranded only in the lot. For a second thought himself inside some other realm of just them teeth and gnashing dark. The journey felt like an assault on his life.

TWENTY-FIVE

It felt like a dream. It landed on her with a great weight. She spent a brief moment just thinking that this is exactly how it happened and how it was just fine being such a way. She did not feel it, not right away. This slipping. She lay in bed for some time. Thought she'd make it to thirty. It seemed centuries away at twenty-seven.

She knew Trasc would leave something. She knew the money had weight to him. Flowers and a letter and a gift. Coffee ready and made. She had a heart. Too much so which would be her end. She stopped going outside. Lugging her body from work to sleep was her only mode of being left to her. She needed a constant to do with not an idea of an aim or the energy to do anything. Her mother was a shell of herself. Felt like that was where she was heading. She wrote to Trasc.

...I went out with my sister. It's been a while. We could barely look at one another. But what I could tell is everything I hate in other people I hated in her. It felt like plastic. Everything wrapped up in pretty little plastic. There is nothing but that hate. I feel like

no matter what we do I will always be filled with something like poison. Thinking on that guy at work. This ride that we're on. Life is a ride and yeah we're on it. Wooo. Hands up. Give me a fucking break. This shit sucks. I can't help but throw my hands up. It feels like we are on the verge of something coming. Like it's all every bit everywhere. Everybody has lost their minds. I just lost heart. Writing this to you feels like a chore. But it's owed to you. Remember when we used to eat together and that would be enough and we would talk for hours. Other day I just threw my hands up at the moment cooking it that one time just sort of like here it is my great moment of the day. I haven't been eating. I feel like I am treading cement. You deserve so much better. Just prepping for my next day I can't finish the task. Laboring over this to ease something I reject. I can call you a friend. My love. I can't stop thinking about it. This certain death...

She had her coffee in silence staring at the wall. She did not bring herself to read the letter. She cried just sitting there blowing on her coffee. Nobody called or texted her besides Trasc at midnight. Second year in a row her mother forgot. Her lingering absence was an absence now. Her sister. No friends.

She sets out to moving around. Opening windows and getting natural light into the house. In no time she's on her hands and knees scrubbing the toilet. It was her first day off in twenty-three days. There was nothing left to listen to. She remains in silence. She cannot comprehend the silence of the place. She started cleaning the house but felt it should feel lived in and begins destroying the place.

TWENTY-SIX

Malachi and Ja take to the hotel bar before checking in. It was busy and right in the middle of hotel rush hour. A game was on that Malachi had no idea how to pronounce the names of teams, but it seemed to attract more patrons. It felt good to be seen. The hearings are on. She can usually pick out a person's politics or if they were police just by how their shoulders sat when they were in that conversation.

"What do you want?"

"I don't know. I'm kind of hungry."

"World smallest bar," Ja leans on it with his palms. The bar is at his waist. "It's what they call it."

"They won't serve us. Blue bar."

"I wouldn't serve you," a man sitting at the bar says.

"Excuse me?" Malachi says.

"Mal, come on."

The man wears NYPD drags.

"Your daddy know who you're out with?"

"You know who her daddy is, Tommy?"

"It's the Wild East now, Steve-O. Them tactics don't work

no more in the playing field. It's not a mob apparatus anymore."

"You sure act like it," Malachi says.

"There's our monkey. Good little monkey."

"A militia with badges."

"We're retired."

"Uns porcos."

"She's got a mouth on her. Look at that. Lucky you. You and my ex-wife speak the same language. You all got an attitude problem. Need that shit tuned a new station."

"Lucky us you're not out on the streets any more so maybe we will give it to you."

"Mal. Come on," Ja brushes her aside.

"I ordered a cheeseburger."

"It's on me," Tommy says. "What room you staying at? I'll bring it up," he smiles. "Man. The pussy these kids get. And they still fucking complain. Talk about diversity."

Mal spits in Tommy's face. He reacts instantly getting up from his stool and knocking over his glass. It shatters. He wraps a hand around Mal's throat and pushes her against the wall. Ja is pounding on the man but he is large. The other man holds him at bay just laughing. Tommy wipes the spit off his face and takes his finger and sticks them in Mal's mouth wiping her spit back on her tongue. She bites down on his fingers and he pulls it away.

"You should swallow that. Never know when the final drop might come."

His breath is warm and smells of cinnamon. Malachi slips out from underneath his arms and her and Ja run off. Tommy watches them as they go.

TWENTY-SEVEN

She makes a cake fashioned out of what she can in the house everything wrecked. Slim picking, she settles on some eggs and a banana. Some cocoa powder and coconut sugar and honey. Strawberries. Makes pancakes with it. Sticks a candle inside and lights it. It all feels arduous. Feeding herself has become toilsome and it all tasted the same. What was she to do, stare at a screen? She sits with a loaded gun.

She didn't want to implicate Trasc in any way. But she liked the feel of the thing. She sings happy birthday to herself in a small, weak voice. The ballad of Eudora, shrill and untuned.

She gets up and tries to dance in the kitchen. She used to do this as a child. In college. When she met Trasc. She once felt truly alive and with the gall and gumption to tackle the world. She felt it drained from her. Had not realized she had stopped moving and was alone in her thoughts just standing still there on the kitchen floor looking at the ground and the mess with shrunken shoulders. She looks at the clock. Nine in the morning. It terrifies her how early it is.

She takes the note and puts it in her pocket. There is a

snarl at the front gate and from where she stands she sees it. Puts her sneakers on and heads out.

A black bear is at the gate. Eudora stands frozen. Surrenders the keys to the castle. It had created some space and Eudora takes direct but slow steps and opens the gate. She moves slowly out into the sounds of the distant train as if moving on to a new lover the bear letting her pass undisturbed and observing her. The sound of the horn blowing loud and hard.

TWENTY-EIGHT

He could not turn off his tired eyes. Felt pretty good. Drank some lemon tea with ginger. Vitamin C after each drink. Match each drink with water of the same volume. Should be good. Ready to go on another bottle. Seven in the morning. He was hammering away for those one hundred dollars all day.

Men at the bar. Trasc dealt with them before. Weren't bad people. Trasc got off and unashamedly walked up to the bar and ordered a double whiskey. Needed directions someplace. Laughed by the way of how in these scenarios on these coasts people will be yelling and screaming but you ask for directions and everybody has an opinion and stops the chatter.

They were cops. One of them going through a divorce. Been staying there a year or so. Trasc kicked the shit with him sometimes. They are disheveled and agitated. He always wears glasses. They're not on his face and his eye is swollen. Trasc was probably asleep when whatever might have happened did. He could care less.

When Trasc rounds about to the suite by the exit he is

surprised to see the sign in sheet moved. Not only moved. Burned. Ashes all over the floor. He hadn't noticed anybody come in. Thought it was his night. The door was already open. He pushes his way in.

To be exposed to so much death. It released things inside of you that are snatched and taken and never gotten back. This seemed as though a feeling that was never going to end.

TWENTY-NINE

"I hate hotels," Ford leans on the window looking in the glass and takes a bite from a banana. The suite is three doors down. "This one isn't even lit right. I feel like I'm going to get cancer just walking in them. I used a towel once after a shower and a tree grew from my back. A fucking tree. My face took on the color some wicked pesto blotched with gnocchi. I have pictures," Ford throws away the banana and takes out his phone.

"This is ridiculous," Trasc says.

"What?"

"No, I don't want to see pictures. How you talking this way to me right now? What's at our feet."

"It ain't in front or at. It's behind. Done happened. Waiting to catch up again. Trying to outrun a bloodhound here, kid. Don't got the legs for it. I have to consider if I really need what I drop on the ground these days. The things you find that you can grow okay with leaving behind. Least we can't forget what it is we cannot remember any such form of our attachments to. It only fit our present moments these sorts of things occupied. I'm saying is you think I got enough

164

tears in this fat head to cry for every murdered Jim and Janice? I wake to the sound of distant hacking because here I am asked to believe somehow there can be any justice in fixing just one of these things. It's not fixing anything. God's janitors."

Trasc blows in his hands.

"There isn't nobody we can call?"

"It costs money."

"I know."

"I don't get wrapped up with them. And you don't have the money."

"Yeah."

"Why did you guys do this? Why not just stay at home?"

"You get desperate. Try and do things for them."

"It doesn't make any sense."

"It's always just trying to find something to do."

"Does John know?"

"I didn't know she even had a key. You don't think it's your guy?"

"No."

"John is going to burn this place to the ground."

"I don't know. Bit of a pacifist now. He isn't weak. It's all been growth and progress."

"Perfect box. We made it for him."

"I don't think this is him. Think of swallowing one every time I come across one of those things. Every one of them. There's a war at hand and we don't see it. I imagine I'll pull a muscle trying to pull the trigger. Sometimes you have to not be greedy and call an end to a night that drags on," something in Ford's indignation changes. "I'm not sure the wood is of this earth. Them boxes."

"What?"

"Nothing. Tent cities out there. We need to draw that up if we are looking in. Talk to the residents and the landlord.

Neighboring rooms. Whoever was at the bar. You worked overnight?"

"Yeah."

"You're loaded."

"Yeah."

"You check anyone in?"

"Everything is pretty much done when I get in. I'm just a guy. I should have known. I should have done something."

"Spare us the loathing shit. I got to stay here tonight and they got no towels. Said a guy didn't wash them."

"How does this work? What we're doing."

"People seem to be licensing lots of things these days. Cash trading hands for unqualified assistances."

There is a tent outside in a corner near a small picnic table and a tree that grows small black things that drop and litter the earth, repeating this cycle. Out of the tent walks a naked man.

"These people. We are dealing with a proliferation of illnesses. I'm not sure I say that with sympathy anymore. They do it to themselves."

Ford walks over to the man and brings him in and gives him a room. Steps back inside the suite.

"She has a broken neck. Our young man shot in the head. Got that right?"

"Unfortunately."

"Stop doing that."

"Doing what?"

"Looking around like that. Using your head. You got eyes. Got to learn to move your eyes."

"World makes it so you don't got much use for them."

"You don't need to look around. Just think and sit somewhere. Sober up. You need to be exposed to this stuff."

"It's all it's ever been."

THIRTY

While Ford canvases tent city Trasc waits in the hotel lobby for his manager to get in. They blocked off the room and any passage to it. Covered the bodies. Trasc wondered what you take with you if anything at all when you cross over in the big exit.

He walks in like a traveling merchant looking hungover and like he just rolled out of bed. Those types that have never done any type of hard service on this sphere.

"Hey, Pablo."

"Adonis, what are you still doing here?"

"I told Nyhim that I would stay on until you got here. Something happened."

He tells him and by no account does it seem to be of easy service staying awake. He considers that this is not the first time something like this has happened under his professional guide. Not the first of the dead among these shallow halls. As Trasc is talking, Pablo is moving around and looks at his phone. Scans his key to the door that takes him behind the front desk. Trasc is going over the night and the what to dos and Pablo keeps on moving.

"Can you stop," Trasc says. "Just stand still for a second when I'm talking to you. Please."

"Why aren't the sheets done?"

"What?"

"The sheets. Why aren't they done?"

"I got here and it was a murderous rage of cotton in there. Nobody did anything. It fell on me. I checked everybody in. Kept a humble, welcoming, likable service and presence here at hours nobody much seems to be awake other than people doing shit like what we got here. Did as much as I can. Dealt with this. I was tired. Sometimes fatigue takes you in the night and you just can't keep folding. I'm here, man. All things considering, you should be thanking me."

"I don't pay you to be on your computer all night."

"You barely pay me at all."

"What is this?" Pablo picks up an empty wine bottle left on one of the folding stations.

Trasc had forgotten about it. He usually does a pretty good job at covering his habits. The fluorescent lights in the laundry mat hang ruthlessly pressing down on them. Pablo sniffs it and pours it over to claim its emptiness.

"What the fuck is this?"

"That's what you want to look into right now? I need to see some tapes, Pablo."

"Get out. You're fired."

"I need those tapes."

"No. Out."

Trasc's about ready to spit out his tongue because the gum of it has lost its taste a long time ago. Grits his teeth.

"You had trouble filling this position. I am consistent and with dignity and am pretty fucking overqualified. The shit I put up with. Deal with here. Every complaint falls on you."

"You're fired."

"Fuck you. I quit."

THIRTY-ONE

Ford had Micah cuffed to the cross and freed the man tied up on it about five minutes into talking to him. That's about all he needed to get all he needed from people. Drew his Glock and had the two lackies backing Micah bring him to who it was that he needed to talk to. Took all about five minutes for him to need a break from it.

Not from the sordidness of this tract but the people within it. This wasn't a looking down on them but rather within. He didn't like what was in there. Didn't like that it made him feel grateful for John's kid not having to be a part of it. A part of what was coming and what is. These young people these days were southbound right here centerfold.

He made his way to the margins of the small encampment to catch some fresh air. Whatever this place had to offer up of such. Opens a can a sardines he won off somebody for some dinner. Opens it and ends up giving it to a stray cat.

It was something edging inspiring. The deleterious modes of being each new generation indelibly lugged themselves around in. They seem to have removed themselves from the Karmic wheel and instead as cutters and knives been placed here somewhere outside eternity only his eyes can see in such detriments of sloth and divorced time to these intestate incorporeal beings of some other kind. To them they wish to exit this suffering which they cannot seem to forfeit or identify. They have deserted themselves and fortified an unconsciousness that leaves them butchered and put off to sleep and somehow still seem intelligible enough to live inside a dream state they have concocted. It's hard to believe that they are human at all. He marvels at the non-difference of their daylight and nocturnal ethereal existences. There is no distinction between their waking self and the dream state. They solve their own problems in example by hallucinating compresences. Doomed imbeciles venerated united rebels with no link to any history or blood in thirsty nimbus piety.

He watches the cautionary tale of this stray picking at the can. Looking about frantic for any incoming predators. No peace to this meal. An offering spent with the possibility of butchering. What a thing to live like that. The cat scrapes the tin dry. Looking about her for any marauder to ruin the blessed meal and this hunger and this fear going on forever. The thought of being predestined to prey animal hide looms over him. Eaten alive. What's that they say about the gnashing of teeth. He supposes it awaits all the living. Ford backs away. Walks these streets of tent city. The ground is muddy and looks wet but is frozen and breaks under his boots.

Floating in this sea of the insane, ill, stupid, depressed, desensitized, neurotic, murderous, or a culmination of all the above somewhere in the middle he liked to believe there might be something like grace. He's about ready to leave. Hasn't gotten any solid information. Barely a solid sentence out of people.

"You like a detective of something," a small kid with long hair says stroking a fire that gives way to being only molten ash. He has a shirt on that says front and back on it.

"Or something," Ford says.

They go on to talking but more so the kid just doing the jabbering. Ford lets him. His eyes and mind were swimming. There was nothing to be found here. Nothing to be solved. No hope repeating. Sees in it that the kid's got nobody to do such a thing with and thinks that it might be good for him.

"You like, figure stuff out and shit," the kid just keeps laughing at nothing.

"Yeah..."

"So like what you going to do with Micah."

"I'm not here for him. I..."

"Did you see what we did to that horse?"

"Kid, I..."

"It wasn't..."

"Kid. You don't let nobody finish what they're saying. You can't sit still and you're all la-la-goo-goo eyed. You don't look healthy. Don't look like you stepped into the sun your whole life. You can't look me in the face and I got more hair than you and probably just about triple your years. I know your head runs circles around you, I do, but you just need to make it sound up there. Be of sound mind. You have the power to do that. Look. I'm shot and I'm gone. You got something to tell me or what. Something I can use."

"There's this guy."

"A guy."

"Yeah. Big guy. Kind of strange. Kind of quiet."

"Shit, kid. Really narrowing it down for me here."

"He don't come much. Don't say much. When he come around folks go missing. Like together people. Folks who are in love, man. We got that here. He always leaves these... these boxes. All about arming people. Most people around here got their guns or ammunition from him. Says the big one coming."

Ford feels gut shot before the kid becomes the very epitome of it. A rifle crack. He watches the red bloom in the kid's belly as if the red in his eyes drains and fills this hole that too is his depletion and whatever color there might have been left paired to those dilations drain out.

Ford turns in the direction he heard the shot. Another one. He sees the muzzle flash come from a window at the top floor of the hotel. His slowness made him feel irresponsible. Unprepared for this moment. He breaks for the building in false galloping, running as fast as he can. People were laughing all about in tent city. Cheering on the events.

The door he exited the building is a stairwell. Right by the room where Mal and Ja are slain. He's yelling for Trasc. Already up the first flight of stairs taking two at a time. Needs to stop and hunch over and catch his breath. His heart pumping and his neck and back tightening.

There are no rooms. No empty spaces. Only tunnels and walls. Moving through the dizzying distortion. All that remains of his will is to collide with all that is to come. Up and up and up the contorting stairs. One flight then another and another.

Light at the end of the tunnel piercing the final door. Top floor. He nearly tumbles over the heavy thickness of it pushing his way by. The musty air floods his lungs like something solid. Cold sweat runs down his back. Salt stings his eyes and seasons his lips. His heart in a state of acidic devolving in his chest.

Down the hall loud metal music drums from a room. A time people should be sleeping. Nobody pays it any mind. Potpourri hanging in small boxes from the ceiling. He pinches back the slide and checks the chamber and aims his pistol moving down the hall slowly. Follows the slow controlled rhythm of the remembered passage to the beat of his heart in order to tame it.

"Whoever is pregnant with evil... the trouble they cause recoils on them; their violence comes down on their heads..."

The sounds of sex. It bothers him such a thing can be taking place amongst these other things. He pans his eyes as he continues to move down the hall towards the music. Some doors have been left open. A woman rides a man as a child sits at the foot of the bed with his eyes glued to the television. A woman snorts cocaine off a desk. A man too bloated to rise from the floor in total filth. Ford moves forward. Reaches the door taking the wall and peels off it kicking the door open and checking the corners. Then he drops to his knees.

"Oh my God."

Ford drops his Glock and begins to pray.

PART 3

THIRTY-TWO

The truth of things came quickly. The things he will be without. The changes that he can't keep up with. Not being able to survive this. There are other roads. He will be faced with shame. Shame has many places he doesn't want to go. Small things that Eudora would handle. He had taken complete advantage and control of her at one point by abuse and manipulation that he figured there was a lonely road someplace he would have to walk all the way up to the bitter end. There never came a time he welcomed death. He feared it and judgement.

Trasc still never got a suit or tie and he wore a black t-shirt with jeans to Eudora's funeral. He had sort of procrastinated the thing off. As if he would be able to explain it to her. He wanted to blow his brains out. This life will kill you in your sleep. The weather felt nothing but falling skies.

When Trasc was younger a boy died at his local high school. A football star he didn't know because Trasc never went. He did attend the funeral to take in certain mannerisms of such a certain kind of loss. He wasn't proud of that. The boy's death was some sort of an attraction. People showing up by the hundreds fold. Lines wrapping down main roads. Everybody passing by on the road aggravates him. As if their day should continue. His world ending. There were four people including the priest here today to see Eudora off.

The day plays tricks. A piercing brightness. Very clear and clean, paired with a bitter cold. The wind is strong though the cemetery has its way of putting a cap on all sound taking everything in its control. The trees rattle away birdsong. A highway is muted just a few yards away respecting the dead over the collection of stone.

Daniella and John did not come. Nobody has seen much of them. It all felt so small. So meaningless. Ford had a heart attack and was in and out. Nobody was caught. Nobody was even looking in on it.

Trasc wanted to see if the cameras were working and they were just fine. Anywhere he went there was some kind of small group. Sometimes nobody. Sometimes one. Coming up with their theories or blames. What they did and what has become of all this became something of a national story. They'd be over it quick.

"It is what it is. Stupid bitch," Rich says. He hits a flask.

There's something of an explosion inside of Trasc's head when he hears it.

Somebody does get on Rich but it only gets him going more.

"It is what it is. You know what I mean? It is what it is."

Trasc is on him and they are rolling down a hill. He wraps his hands around his throat. People are calling and running down after them.

"Say it again," Trasc is hysterical and crying. "I WANT YOU TO SAY IT AGAIN. IS TAKING YOUR LIFE HARD WORK ENOUGH FOR YOU?"

A dog is barking upon the funeral. Hounding siren of a car. Hands on Trasc as people try to pull him off of Rich.

Thick veins lacing around Trasc's forearms. Rich's pupils are the size of ink blots.

"Get out of my fucking way."

Trasc is raised up and off him. Thrown to the ground when he gives some retention. He rolls, taking the earth in stride. On his feet. Ford stepping before him.

"Walk," Ford says hammering forward.

Trasc steps up. Heavy hands on his chest and he is thrown to the dirt again. Trasc thinks it's road by the feel of it and the cold. He scrambles and gets back to his feet retreating steps this time.

"I'll walk you like a dog," Ford takes out brass knuckles. Puts them on. "Walk."

Trasc backs away onwards past an embankment of dead trees over hills of brown grass and small rivers and leaves like sharp things. The sky looks fattened in its emergence. Something like swinging fists in the air. Ford stops on top of the hill.

"It was a woman. Victoria."

"What?"

"Looking for you. Hired people like us."

"People like us."

"Yeah."

"Thanks."

"Trasc."

Trasc flicks his head.

"Do something else."

"There's nothing else."

Ford fades away into changing sun like a record repeating, cycling in the sky.

THIRTY-THREE

There was a fox. She knew it to be a fox. A mother fox crying out in the expanse of sparse woodland surrounding the neighborhood. Her own mother told her stories about mother foxes looking for their children lost in the woods when she was a girl. Told Daniella that if anything ever happened to her, she would rescue her.

Daniella lay on the cold hard floor for days gone by. Sleep has become her divinity. She hasn't seen John in what has been something of about three months. It amazes her because he is just outside, just out back. He's laboring on at something unknown to her.

What amazed her was the memory of how many times before they'd been together but so alone. He'd be rapping in the basement and she would be reading in bed upstairs and sometimes they would go days without speaking or seeing one another. Nothing nefarious, just a thought. And it was those thoughts, those thoughts of having, that made the vanishment feel as though a whole color had been erased.

Each and every day has brought about a climate that

created meteorological pressures on the banausic coordinates surrounding her incumbency.

The same time every night it calls in the distance. She gets up from off the floor. Certain days where she sits long enough rising on her feet feels as though she strikes a match and swallows it. Her blood slow muddy trails of gasoline within her. She imagines this might have been the way Malachi felt. On days no other reason at all but the day itself. It seemed to be of forced registry. That the days come upon them like rabid animals or mortars coming from some great unknown dropping on them the moment they wake up one after the other like a war where mercy costs lives. It wasn't so hard when she was young. But she wasn't here when she was young. She imagined it to be just about the same for their young people. Until they had more young people. Like a cycle that needed closing. A crime that kept on being committed that needed solving. This place was no longer her home. She should be extradited and held accountable.

Of sound mind but only that of the sound of screaming. Her body feels frail and weak. The fox nominates her losses to the wind calling for her lost children. Tonight it is louder than before. She steps outside into snow barefoot and follows the trail by sound. Stumbles upon the fox as its cries grow more faint and it dies where it stands of her sorrow.

"Daniella."

She turns and John stands before her.

"I'm sorry."

"You said that you would keep us safe. This is unsacred land. Our babies. It's not right. Not right having daughters. You know what you do to them. Both of them. Oh, Johnny. Both."

THIRTY-FOUR

John pulls up to the hotel and grabs his supplies from the trunk of his car. His first intention was to build back up the derelict church adjacent from the Circle. Certain kinds of loss makes new plans on how to go about coping with the rest of your life. Like some great task that requires a clocking in and enduring up until the very end.

John begins his work. He commissions in the dark and the cold, exposed to the spray paint. He breathes it in. There is an image in his head that he cannot see to this brick canvas as his artistic vision is blurred by all his failures flooding his eyes.

He had painted the same thing on the first house to the right upon entering the circle adjacent from the church. He knows the man inside. The soft, average man, skating through life and his marriage and his fatherhood. John was still hard at his age and looked the one thing that did not belong in every room that he was in. Like his looks and certain power and confidence in his presence determined something more than what was to be had within the constructs of those around him with their shitty diets, their laziness, their mindsets. Their weaknesses. These sorts of people made him sick. Breathing the same air as them tasted bad in his mouth.

"The fuck you think you're doing," the man said exiting his house and meeting John on the side. "Jesus. John. I didn't know it was you. I'm sorry. What happened. If there's anything we can do."

"Anything you can do. Can I do this? To your house? Huh? Is it worth that much? How's about when I'm done I head inside and fuck your wife properly. Fuck out of here. This is my neighborhood."

It is far from perfect, but it is done. He backs away and examines the graffiti mural of his daughters. The frailty in the chest, nothing as the skull. It was easy to mine the images inside of his heart more so than the head. He had sued the NYPD before over a graffiti cleanup. Called the piece "Death from Above." John wrote the report himself.

"Using an undiscerning eye and an obtuse brush, the untrained crew went out to blot out art from street canvases, violating the artists' protections under free speech and copyright laws..."

New York's finest at the 84th precinct practiced their unceremonious erasing. Never finding his daughter's killer then ridding her memory. John drops to his knees. Places a hand on the hotel and tries to pray. He wanted to start with a five and ten but cannot remember the words to the two simple prayers so he makes his own to what sounds like vengeance. He repeats their names until he loses his voice.

———

John hacks away at the last remaining trees in his yard. Drags them to the backyard and begins his drudgery.

"Sorry to interrupt," Ford says.

"That's all anybody says these days. All anybody ever says. Sorry. Everybody's so fucking sorry."

"Daniella said I would find you back here. She's leaving, John."

The men stand in silent benediction.

"And so am I," Ford says. John just looks in the dirt. "Ro is pregnant. Shit. I don't know if I should congratulate or console these days on that when somebody tells me," John keeps on the ground. "Anybody can just fuck anybody into existence. No charge and nothing asked. No qualifications. As if you're somebody worth being around. As if they have a sustainable future. It seems a hijacking of consciousness to me. Birth," John wouldn't be much for the antinatalism right now. "We all know what you said, John."

"Wow."

"I don't want to know what you did."

"You motherfucker. I will bury you back here. Do you fucking hear me? Bury you. Say what you said was shit. Say it. Say what you say is fucking shit."

"John..."

John takes out a 1911 from the base of his spine. Ford draws his Glock.

"Get on your fucking knees and beg me to forgive what you just said to me."

"The fuck you doing out here then, John?" Ford points at a ladder weighed down deep in thick, wet grass. Yard fence has been knocked down so that it can stretch out.

"Building a ladder."

"I see that."

"To God. I'm building a ladder to God so I can kick his fucking teeth in."

"Won't reach."

"I'll knock out the sun then."

"That bulb's been flickering."

"You don't know nothing, asshole. This is a place people have fucking amnesia."

"There are still private systems. If they want to look."

"They won't find shit. Because I didn't do shit. This isn't about me."

"They won't be the best. Won't like work. It's why I don't like flying. Doctors are even no good."

"Well then I will take a look."

"The kid is a piece of shit."

"Who."

"This Lott guy."

"No."

"Do it for your daughters. I'll show you some things. You'll change your mind."

"Don't talk about my daughters."

"Give me a break, John."

The men put down their weapons.

"The hell can I do for them. You motherfucker. What the hell can I do for them? He's punishing me for my sins. This shit cannot happen twice to a person or this world ain't worth nothing for nobody and I'll go on a spree myself and not stop until all of you ungrateful bastards are in the ground and you know I'm good for it and I'll burn this whole fucking world to the ground as Satan roamed the earth back and forth and back and forth and back and forth. You fucking hear me."

"If you're being punished, John, who is punishing your girls?"

"They're dead."

"Who condemned them to such a fate? Or are they not worthy of your God? Not you. Too much service."

John is writhing.

"If God is punishing you, he's punishing you for having them. Now that they're gone and you've been punished, and in their taking they have been punished, who punishes God for the taking? This isn't about you. Looking for an ear up there. Anywhere here. You're left unsatisfied in speaking and lonely in the silence. He taught us that language of forlorn defeatism."

"This Lott guy. You're telling me the type of man that he is. Type of father."

"It's not good, John. That kid is being born in trenches."

"What kind of father am I? Huh? What kind of fucking father am I? You tell me."

"John. Only thing you buried back here was yourself all them years ago. Looks like you came back from the dead."

"Tell me. Motherfucking cocksucker. You fucking tell me."

"You ain't one no more, John. I'm sorry."

John raises up and shoots Ford in the face. Nobody in the neighborhood pays the shot any attention. John looks up at his house and Daniella watches him from inside behind red lights and rain slick glass. He hears movement inside the house when she's gone and she walks outside with two shovels and drops one at his feet. They dig. She says a prayer and tosses a shovelful inside the small pit and leaves the rest to him.

THIRTY-FIVE

When Daniella is back inside there is a woman standing right in the entryway near the stairs looking off into the dining room to her left. She stands epileptic and strange staring and not moving with no regard of Daniella at all. She does not touch anything. Does not look away from the same spot.

"Is that where it happened?" Daniella says.

The woman does not speak.

"I know about you. About this home. What happened. People talk. I'm sorry," Daniella moves into her ear. "Get out of my house. This is not your curse. You don't get to take away my tragedy."

———

She wondered at what point one must decide to deal with the consequences of your actions and how one might regard fighting for their home and by what bounds. Then she landed on that she did not have a home. Not one she'd call such. She felt determined to begin again. To be something greater than the sum of her grievances and injuries and plunders.

Daniella had walked the trail and felt its orchestration as a dance. A way of taking in the entirety of the grounds. Made sure of no signs of life then checked again and reflected upon her own and all the webs growing inside there instead holding it all together, leaving behind homes, and gathering in the memories.

She packed lightly. Did not want anything to weigh her down in her gravitational departure. All the burners were set. She lights the match and walks out into a cold that will forever vanquish the abdominal heat. If anything at all she no longer wanted to feed this violent, sycophantic, nihilistic wasteland any longer. These people were never satisfied, unappreciative, didn't listen, classless, and overfed. Most of all they didn't pray.

She rarely saw grace around a table, veteran of the business. Cannot recall a time around her own. It was no longer her tab, her debt. She'd been collecting them. Considers the fire to her back burning a past life that she'll never look back upon and hopes that it will consume the entire country. Her days at this moment have no meaning but she had the will to trek those tumultuous travels and find a way to better.

When the table is set she folds her hands and thinks of what she will say. She looks around at the lonely place. Food started becoming more expensive. All together it just became hard to get. The restaurant slowly receding from being out of this and that to being out of everything. Behind all the schemes and veils the food shortages. You would look around and hardly be able to tell. Her gratitude has become thoughts of betrayal. She thinks of murdered traditions and all the tables of one. Holidays she's made them work. Thanksgiving and Christmas. She thinks of all the lonely meals John had.

Talked this whole thing in motion. She begins to cry and throws a wineglass at the wall. It was like this place had stolen her grace.

The comfort in the mere thought that we do not live forever. She considers the French way of thinking any act of suicide being pointless because any act of suicide was too late. She figures she will break the chains and fortify a woman with a resolve she would have wished the girls to live by. Cut out what society and this life and this grief has intended for her and live for something more. She could feel her eyes burn like hot coals never to see happiness again. You need to think of yourself as the one and only. The one and forever only. She has heard everything John has to say. This grief would bring with it a boredom she would not be able to survive. She had to outlive it, outrun it, and find something new.

THIRTY-SIX

Trasc was at the bottom of a bottle. It was propped up right next to him. His head down on the bar in his folded arms. He would pop up from time to time and have himself a bit of hydration.

"Your glasses are fixed," Trasc says through slurred words.

"Yeah," the man down the bar says.

"What was it again?"

"Steve."

"That's right."

Trasc goes on drinking and the men keep going on talking.

"There were two of you that night."

"What?"

"Small world."

"Buddy. Beat it."

"Somebody said you were upset that night. With the victims. Had some words."

"She was mouthing off. You think I'm afraid to talk to you? Nobody gives a shit."

The truth to the matter under those dim lights. There was

nobody around to listen. The story of his life was the story of the bottle. A tragic and utter idleness. That was what it seemed to become. A five year or so blackout. Steve gets up and walks off. Trasc swings around in his booth and falls belly up on the ground. The room was spinning complete circles around him.

There was nothing left now but to wreck terrible and exact havoc on himself. To obliterate any sense of moral compass or restraint. No such thing as commitment or responsibility. There would be nobody to hold him accountable. Indulgence and detachment would become a way of life.

THE PEOPLE OF THE STATE OF NEW JERSEY,
PLAINTIFF,

-VS-   CASE NO. ████████

████████ DEFENDANT

REPORTER'S TRANSCRIPT OF PROCEEDINGS
MARCH 10, 2033

APPEARANCES:

FOR THE PEOPLE: ████████
                                   DEPUTY DISTRICT ATTORNEY

FOR THE DEFENDANT: N/A

OFFICIAL COURT REPORTER: ████████
                                   C.S.R. NO. 10907

HOPATCONG, NEW JERSEY   MARCH 10, 2033

PROCEEDINGS (27 OF 27)

MR. TRASC: Imagine that a place. You have no way out and no options. You are in donzoville. Fell for the wrong blah, blah. And you're more upset than ever with blah, blah. And she could give two shits. You're fucked. This is the beginning of the end. I couldn't believe it. How do you not see warning signs or flashing red lights when you get together for something like Christmas and can't tell if it's a funeral or a holiday. No fun. No joy. No grace. It was so miserable and so horrible and so terrifying that I felt it starting to change me. Change the others in the room. Like all of a sudden I wasn't the only one to watch the sun burn out. I haven't met very many people who had similar holidays. Then it seemed everyone was having them. These are things lost in measuring gradations. Coming home all around the same time our shit happened I remember leaving early because I just couldn't be around that sort of thing much longer. There was a stop. It was on the wire of the strike but police were still around and some guy cut up his father into a mess because they had a heated exchange. Holiday Homicide they were calling it. They'd been living with his mother and sister, too. Well he just cut him up and there was screaming and then the silence and they went looking for that boy and they found him. They all the town hung red lights the rest of that long winter. It felt like a premonition. Like a warning of not things to come but where we already were and where we'd been heading and just how there's nothing coming at all after this and what we've done to ourselves. Everybody is so cold. So detached. So jaded. I seen this take a toll on Eudora. Had the opposite take on me. I felt like running towards grace. Looking for peace. I didn't know what that meant but I felt it and I needed it. Just running up into brick walls. She never gave me any credit for that. For watching her get run over seeing them lights barreling down and having nothing that can be done about it but wait out the bleed. You ever wonder what if it's as hard to get into heaven as it is into the hall of fame? Ah. Forget it. Figuring I'm on about nothing again. I guess you just letting me do all the talking here. She'd do that. I'd be talking and she'd just sit there taking the punches saying I'm talking to myself and just wait for me to finish and she's already made up her mind. She never had nothing to say. We measure the intentions and mold and warp them to our own complexities and pasts and triggers.

THE COURT: Sounds dire.

MR. TRASC: I think it is. She was stunned by her own potential. I think I started to believe in sickness as a way of carrying someone off. Growing desperate from the fight and ultimately giving up or giving in for surely anything was better than this. She'd be the one not to bend at the knee. I left the hotel that night all bent out of shape and everything just shot to total hell and man the rings just kept spinning. Went home and the door was slightly open. Saw the money and the note and I just took on running up the road barefoot towards the sound of the train. Barefoot because my boots were all worn and wet and cold. Mainly because of the blood on them. Sitting in the empty house that night just holding an old dress of hers in my arms it was every bit a last drink effort there. Last stand. I remember the dress. It was white with red polka dots on it that now just looks to me like bullet holes thinking back on it. For so long I just wanted to hold her. Now I just want to forget her so I don't need to feel this way anymore. Come back here. Anchored my heart. It all ends the same. Need to be superman to dodge that bullet.

THE COURT: How so.

MR. TRASC: Less about it the better. We left her alone to fight for her life and pushed her into a corner where she could use her strengths to prove us something. She was left with the fact that all she had was the suicide. It was in the sermon, Joan put it. I remember the look in her eyes sometimes. Sometimes she just felt so deeply. Everybody just trying to be together when we first came up. Looking to be at odds. She said crying with profound hunt for reason as to why we were not all laughing and having a good time together. I'm sorry. I just miss her so much.

THE COURT: I'm sorry.

MR. TRASC: I'm sorry about your man. Make you nervous?

THE COURT: I'm volunteer.

MR. TRASC: Aren't we all. Why are you on me so hard about Eudora?

THE COURT: What is the happiest day of your childhood?

MR. TRASC: The day I got the hell out of it.

THE COURT: Yes. But when was this?

MR. TRASC: What does this have to do with anything? I can't answer the question. I don't have an answer. But you do. Why are you bringing up Eudora?

THE COURT: Why do you think that she took her own life?

MR. TRASC: She didn't. She left. She's gone.

THE COURT: You think she's in a better place?

MR. TRASC: I do. She is missing. Not deceased. Not a suspect. She is a missing person. Start treating her as one.

THE COURT: We have been. But her DNA was on that train.

MR. TRASC: That girl. Her DNA is on the moon. So, we are here for entertainment purposes? Reliving old stories.

THE COURT: Pretty much. But I think what is important is that they feel it. I think people, maybe a little bit of our generation, they can't connect.

MR. TRASC: I don't know. I am a little bit dried out on the penchant for human depravity and the awake nihilist ninjas.

THE COURT: The awake nihilist ninjas?

MR. TRASC: Unfortunately, we have them. Philosophical debates amongst your fellows is showmanship. It is creative performances. To hungry people everything is meat. Life is suffering. Blah, blah, blah. Half-truths as susceptible to a self-righteous illusion. Which has led you to this story of crime. That very same hunger. This torrid and kinetic tale infusing timely and important with tragedy, heartbreak, and love. Selves entangled in circumstance. Revelations of language and self under pressure. This cross examination of your crimes into the human spirit in conflict with itself. Ah, don't quote that. The rest you can. That's me. And that's pretty fucking brilliant. Spirit shit, you know the one, that was Faulkner, not me. Despite our kinship as dead men.

THE COURT: You're being funny again.

MR. TRASC: Yeah well, you're not laughing.

THE COURT: I didn't know you felt this way.

MR. TRASC: Multiple truths.

THE COURT: We are trying to get down to one truth here.

MR. TRASC: Every bed we make carries all of our sicknesses. Every clear sky was only ever a mere symptom of our fabrications because in the end it was always the same cold and gray and nothing sky. I know those nights. I know alone. Every single way this body can sin and cast ire out from every rusted pore. I've swam the depths of all our pleasures, ones even the devil himself would sit out on. Who would subject one to such a thing? And yet I have. Nothing but the prosperity in pain. Imagine me or any of us in this not a representation of any flag, gender, race, creed, sex, or age. Only that of the diseased human heart. Think me a nihilist. The bleeding colors of the heart. Alienated all people because what was ever the worth of them. Whatever was there to like in this self-sufficed survival of the most unfit? You tell me. And in that indelible alienation, I feel true nausea at the sight of you. The human face makes me sick. Every breath we take is a crime. I am repulsed by it. We would eat one another just to throw each other up, the French put it. Unmovable and unreachable. This crisis of life. There was never any matter of existentialism, it was always a meager existence, with a penchant for extinction. What does one make of the dead marching on a dying planet.

THE COURT: You can't be serious.

MR. TRASC: You're right. But I think we live in a society that has about that wavelength tuned to their skulls. Looking back on it now. None of us got in any trouble. This whole thing unfolded at a real different angle. I don't even remember anyone being unfaithful. Our intentions were fractured but our executions were pure. Everything starts at the floor mainly of just wanting to have a good time. Wanting to be liberated of all your spoils. We had cycles and legacies of sin that lived on. It seems eternal. In every heart of this story. The what never goes away. The new thing and breed of self-righteous nothingness. People's inability to cope with all the time given to them. That's why we wanted to be courted. Wanted you to bear witness to ourselves.

THE COURT: I just find a distant lack of discipline in the narrative thread and structure.

MR. TRASC: How so.

THE COURT: You could have tried harder. You and everybody involved. This whole thing reads a way that it is not supposed to.

MR. TRASC: That's maybe because you are getting just exactly what you need. I came on as a PI at the time a man was just about on the fritz and end and along that road was a hard road of failures and aftershocks. He did me some favors, but I put in the work.

THE COURT: We never fully established a timeline of when one of the deceased got a key to the room.

MR. TRASC: I am assuming you spoke with John on that.

THE COURT: Use the number in front of you please.

MR. TRASC: Right sorry. Uhm. Number four. Have you spoken with him.

THE COURT: We have.

MR. TRASC: You are not telling the truth about something. Maybe about a few things.

THE COURT: A little hypocritical.

MR. TRASC: I don't hide from my hypocrisies. We are skillful at the way we lie. A natural gift. Won the Trojans the war. Losing your life is not by any means or stretch of these imaginative hearts the end all be all grand climax upon this stage. There are worse things than losing your life, and the worse things are but one. Losing the love in that life. Living to feel this loss of love, cannibalizing any feeling of a loss of life. You must be careful about getting your heart broke. Careful about the hearts you break.

THE COURT: Would you call yourself a sociopath?

MR. TRASC: Look around you. Everybody is a somethingpathicsomething.

THE COURT: Do you feel like your fears are being preyed on?

MR. TRASC: Dostoyevsky said pain and suffering are always inevitable for a large intelligence and a deep heart. Probably fear, too.

THE COURT: You mentioned the Trojan war.

MR. TRASC: The Trojan horse did not die within the walls of Troy. It galloped into the hearts of every man, woman, and child, waiting to burn these bone cities down.

THE COURT: What do you think Paris would say? About the war being worth it?

MR. TRASC: It was. If war and death are inevitable and forever, why not be for love? They would have been on the beaches of Troy sooner or later. It was all because somebody fucked the wrong girl and loved the wrong girl. Look what a broken heart led someone to do. Led us.

THE COURT: Interesting theory.

MR. TRASC: I'm not sure what we are looking for here.

THE COURT: A bit like our Boxman. Leaning into our unknowability as people being people. We solve one thing and another just goes on the distance free right of passage.

MR. TRASC: You haven't told me why you keep bringing up Eudora.

THE COURT: The cycle of violence that descended on you in such a vacuum. It is bizarre to say the least.

MR. TRASC: My boy is starting to look a little familiar over there. Hey, keep it up buddy. Almost done. Great job. Sitting there so still. So quiet. You asked me one of my favorite days as a kid? I had an older brother. Drank himself off a road. Back when we were kids I was always alone. Some kids started getting to making chlorine bombs. Sticking them in mailboxes. Big brother leading the charge. One day a kid throws it inside somebody's kitchen. Kills a little kid inside. Federal agents came to my house grilling my brother just straight up lying to their faces. We were always good at that. Lying.

THE COURT: You should not be saying such stuff in court, Mr. Trasc.

MR. TRASC: I'll never forget his face. He had a very distinct chin. I remember hearing he came back. Became a cop. Saw him on the block a few times as a kid. Tom. It's Tom, right. Man, they let anybody become a cop.

THE COURT: He is here for penance.

MR. TRASC: The second man. You see things recalibrate their shapes contextualizing meaning of each individual thing. You seek definition in stenciled figures. You would wonder what on the last days of your life the mere shapes of objects might mean to you. Inanimate objects. A cup and a tissue box made me cry once I was so alone for so long. You need a hand to hold. That's it. All there is to it. You just do. You go through phases where you don't want to be here or you think you could do it alone and hopefully you come out on it the other side with somebody and providing for other people. Being a mender. Keeper of the peace. You wonder how a human being can be so consumed with despair if just given to them a room and a body. Give them what they need to survive. But what of the great material inside the perfect running that is your consciousness and the system in which your body transports life to your state of being. Think of human senses as tools. We obtain them. If you were sitting in a room, simply smelling things then making stories from those smells in your mind. Is it a drawing or some kind of erasing? We search for answers through work moving on from them as we age and then we simply die. Don't try so hard to create a whirlwind in the ecosystem.

THE COURT: Mr. Trasc. You are here because in large part we are here for a much broader examination. So we appreciate your thinking here. But it is indirect and offensive.

MR. TRASC: What is the examination? There is only a truth in deficiencies unless you have the stamina that would bring you to temptation and failing at fending such off. It's like we all have something at one point and you have it all. Then it becomes the worst. Most relationships lead to a dead end. I think being alone too long really clouds the brain in ways that terrified me. Like contracting CTE from ghosts.

THE COURT: The conundrum of the head versus the heart.

MR. TRASC: You can't be serious.

THE COURT: Pushed through our own personal combine. High functioning nervous breakdowns. You went to a land no man or woman can come back from. The avatar projected collapsed and the struts holding these souls together began to crumble. You look for a place to begin again at the end and rearranging of these vignetting lives.

MR. TRASC: What is this?

THE COURT: Ma'am. You don't need to write this anymore.

<AMENDMENT>

WHAT FOLLOWS IS A TRANSCRIPTION IN LIVE EVENT OF THE PROCEEDINGS. THE TRANSCRIPTION WAS HANDWRITTEN.

"The man seated gets up. Confesses. Manslaughter. He wants a charge of involuntary manslaughter. For everybody. Cops took strike. After the shooting. Paid severance to leave. Confessing. Crying. Killed that girl. That boy. The other guy. Money used for this trial on himself. Door to the room opens. Number four steps into the room. Emotional wreckage. A shaking hand. He aims a gun and suspect begs for his life. Reading verdict. The sound of the end of the world. People screaming. Running outside to see what happened. Bright bright bright. There is a sound that is the end of everything. Hold my hand as I leave this place behind."

The flood had taken most of the coastal plane of New Jersey. He floats on down a causeway looking for lost souls. He built her himself, Euroclydon. The super event has stripped them of their meanings. Standing outside the little courthouse of their private envisioning of reconciliations and atonements while white smoke rose out at sea. At one point he leaves the boat and floats on down the sea as they continue their search in streets that reveal to them no claim of whereabouts at all. He floats on down with his arms and legs outstretched. He is floating on down, focusing on the sun to block out the screams. He thinks to drink up this ever-flowing chalice. Let it all fill up. Jump in, drink up. He collides in his aquatic drifting with another traveler and they embrace and float on down the water together with the rope secured around them. He is crying, adding to this mad river of sanctimony. Last final rage of this. He feels all of his pain, all the guilt, and all the shame washed away in the arms of this stranger. A new trueness of sobriety. His hands and his heart forever at last washed clean. The water filling the spaces of what lay broken inside of him. Shape of an angel, saving grace, taking him in and pulling him aboard. He knows her shape and her wingspan miles away on deck. All the groans pouring out into the water rest in the turmoil of the wonderings of now or always have been, in scripture, are we of the sea or the leviathans rising up from the pit. Everything living carries a soul, just as you. Carrier of souls sail on. Sail on. Sail on.

ABOUT THE AUTHOR

Anthony Gedell writes from New Jersey publishing in *Hobart*, *Poverty House*, *Variant*, and *Punk Noir Magazine*. This is his first novel.